A Note on the Author

Award-winning author Margrit Cruickshank is perhaps best known for her popular S.K.U.N.K. series. *S.K.U.N.K. and the Ozone Conspiracy* was short-listed for the Irish Book Award in 1990. She was short-listed for the Bisto Book of the Year Award in 1991, and again in 1992, and was the winner of the 1993 Reading Association of Ireland Special Merit Book of the Year Award for her young adult novel, *Circling the Triangle*. *Anna's Six Wishes* was short-listed for a Children's Book Award in the UK in 1996 and is on their recommended reading list. Margrit Cruickshank lives and works in Dublin.

S.K.U.N.K.

and the
Nuclear Waste Plot

3

S.K.U.N.K.

and the
Nuclear Waste Plot

3

Margrit Cruickshank

*The third book in an exciting series
that just gets better and better!*

POOLBEG

First published 1992 by
Poolbeg Press Ltd,
123 Baldoyle Industrial Estate,
Dublin 13, Ireland

This edition published 1999

The Arts Council
An Chomhairle Ealaíon

A catalogue record for this book is available from the British Library.

ISBN 1 85371 723 1

Cover design by Artmark
Cover illustration by Leonard O'Grady
Printed and bound in Great Britain by
Cox & Wyman Ltd, Reading, Berkshire.

My thanks are due to Greenpeace, in particular to Helen Kingston, for help in researching the scientific basis for this book. Any mistakes and all opinions are entirely my own.

To Kirsten, Ashley, Louise, Siobhán,
Tanya and Heather

Contents

1

Babysitting

Aisling Daly slammed her mug down on to the draining board. "I don't see why my whole holiday should be wrecked because of Seamus," she complained. "That's almost a week wasted now and you know I was invited down to the Shannon this Easter. It's so totally unfair. And the weather's been fantastic too! Louise and her family must be having a ball down there."

"Life is unfair," her mother pointed out. "And Seamus is your godfather."

"He's Florence's brother. Florence is supposed to look after him, not me. If she'd stayed at home, neither of us would have to put ourselves out like this."

"Really, Ash?" Mrs Daly raised an eyebrow. "How very sweet of you to be concerned about me too. After all, I only spend all night up there—*you* have to look in on him during the day and see to his meals. My heart bleeds for you."

"Sarcasm is the lowest form of wit, mother dear. And it's true. Apart from which Florence is far too old to go off to Britain, campaigning for nuclear disarmament like some sort of geriatric hippy. It's ludicrous."

Mrs Daly sighed. "Sometimes I despair of you, Aisling. Now you're not only being sexist, you're being ageist too.

1

You should be ashamed of yourself."

"Her generation's not supposed to go in for things like that. And anyway, she could at least have waited for Archie to get home from wherever he's gone sailing off to, before she went away. He's her husband, after all. He could have babysat Seamus just as easily as I could."

"Maybe. But he isn't here and you are. So on your bike, young lady, and get up there. Seamus wasn't in great form when I left this morning and he won't be pleased if you're late."

"Blast Seamus!" Aisling muttered. Mrs Daly pretended not to hear.

□

By the time she reached Seamus's house, overlooking Dalkey Hill, Aisling was hot, tired and extremely fed up. She leant her bike against the creeper-covered wall and felt in the pocket of her anorak for the key to the back door.

A miaow, heartbreaking enough to bring tears to the eyes of a fourteen-stone bully, came from high above her head. She ignored it.

There was a crashing sound, like a ten-ton gorilla falling through the top of the jungle canopy, as Mulligan, Florence's huge orange cat, left the ledge outside Florence's bedroom window (where he'd been sitting hopefully since early morning) and plunged down through the clematis to twine himself around her legs.

Aisling pushed him out of the way. "Get off, you great hairy monster. I know Mum fed you before she left, so don't try to pretend you're starving."

Mulligan gazed up at her. He was a cat devoted to his stomach and found it hard to accept that others mightn't rate feeding him their number one priority. As soon as Aisling opened the door, he rushed in to the kitchen and sniffed accusingly at his empty plate.

Aisling grinned at him. "Hard cheese, Mulligan. Did nobody ever tell you that life is unfair? No? Believe me, you're lucky."

She jumped as a piercing whistle came from the speaking tube beside the sink. This tube connected the kitchen with Seamus's studio in the attic and enabled Seamus to pass on his orders to Florence or whoever was in the kitchen; in this case, herself. She wondered how long Seamus had been trying to get hold of her and then decided she didn't care. He could wait until she'd squeezed a couple of oranges and made herself a drink. After all, he wasn't to know she'd arrived yet.

The whistle screeched again, louder this time. At the fourth blast, which was so loud the crockery trembled and Mulligan dived under the table with his ears pressed flat to his head, she gave in. "Yes?"

"And about time too!" Seamus's grumpy voice came down the tube. "You're late this morning. I had to make my own cup of tea."

"Tough," Aisling muttered.

"I heard that. I'd like you to bring up the post before you start making my lunch. Not that there will be anything interesting in it, but I live in hope of life surprising me."

Aisling crashed the speaking tube back on to its holder

3

and went through to the hall. She was delighted to see that there was nothing but brown envelopes lying on the mat. She hoped all the bills were huge.

As she climbed the two flights of stairs to the attic, Mulligan streaked past her and skidded to a stop outside Seamus's door. She grinned and let him in. Seamus hated Mulligan coming into his room: it was about time someone made him suffer for a change.

Her godfather was an invalid, confined to a huge brass bed in the middle of the attic studio. He was an inventor as well as an artist and his inventions helped him to cope with his disability. A table beside his bed held an array of switches which operated mechanical arms; these moved his easel to where he could reach it, handed him paints or paper, opened or shut the skylight window, worked the "teasmade" machine or operated the pulley which connected with the kitchen and by means of which Florence (or, at the moment, herself, Aisling thought bitterly) could send up his food.

She followed Mulligan into the room and watched with satisfaction as he leapt on to the bed and collapsed, purring loudly, across Seamus's legs, his long orange body stretching like a furry draught-excluder from one side of the bed to the other.

Seamus gave him a filthy look, swung the painting he'd been working on out of the way, looked pointedly at his watch and glared at Aisling. "What kept you? It's practically afternoon."

"It's only eleven-thirty."

"It's eleven-thirty-four-and-a-half. And you're supposed to be here by ten. You didn't arrive till ten-thirty two

4

days ago and yesterday it was eleven. By the time Florence comes home, it'll be midnight before I have the dubious pleasure of your company. If you're still coming at all."

Aisling shrugged. "I thought I was supposed to make your meals and be around in case you needed me. I didn't think I had to babysit you all day long."

"Babysit?" Seamus puffed up like a cobra, his face flushing an alarming shade of red. Aisling wondered what you did if someone had a heart attack. She wished Mr Cassidy taught them first aid instead of bookkeeping at school: it would be far more useful.

"You know what I mean," she said quickly. "Look after you when Florence is away."

"Babysit!" Seamus repeated. He no longer looked as if he was going to burst, just as if he'd like to strangle her. "Babysit! What do you think I am? Some mewling, puking babe in nappies that you have to mollycoddle and look after every hour of the day?"

Aisling decided not to remind him that that was just what he had been complaining about: she hadn't been around to look after him every hour of the day. "Here's your mail," she said instead, thrusting the pile of brown envelopes at him.

He glanced impatiently through them and added them to a heap of other unopened brown envelopes which lay on the floor beside his bed. "Florence can deal with these when she comes back."

"When is she coming back?" Aisling asked. "Have you heard from her?"

Seamus frowned. "No."

5

Aisling wondered if it was a letter from Florence he'd been expecting. "She's been gone almost a week, hasn't she? You'd have thought a letter would have reached Ireland by now."

"She's probably too busy to write. If I know Florence, she'll be organising the whole camp, running up diet sheets, cooking meals, darning clothes, minding babies... I'm sure all these liberated women she's with haven't the foggiest idea how to look after themselves."

He's jealous, Aisling thought. He'd behaved just like a spoilt child when Florence had married Archie the previous autumn (after they'd come back from Iceland where they'd stopped the evil gang called S.K.U.N.K. from splitting the world apart). And now Archie had gone off on another long sailing trip with Thorwald, and Florence had abandoned Seamus to be looked after by Aisling and her mother and gone to protest against nuclear bombers or something.

"I wish Florence had told me she was going to Greenham Common," she said. "I'd have loved to go with her."

"Greenham Common!" Seamus snorted. "Trust you to get it wrong. If someone organised an expedition to the North Pole, you'd end up in Africa."

"That's not fair. Any time I've gone off with you, chasing S.K.U.N.K., I've been as much of a help as anyone else."

"S.K.U.N.K....Hmm. Yes." Seamus drew the easel towards him again and stared gloomily at it. Aisling looked too. She expected to see one of Seamus's usual Irish landscapes and was startled to find that he was

6

painting a picture of a huge grey factory with a high wall round it and the kind of globe-shaped buildings that she associated with pictures of a nuclear power station. In the foreground was a huddle of tents with people sitting on the grass having a picnic. Only it wasn't the sort of cheery afternoon-by-the-river-in-spring-type picnic that you get in French impressionist paintings: the sky was full of heavy grey clouds, the tents were black and threatening, the people seemed cold and miserable and very worried.

As she looked, Seamus took a brush, dipped it in black paint, and, with a few deft strokes, sketched in two more figures at the other side of the foreground, positioning them out of sight of the campers behind some bushes. Aisling drew in her breath sharply: Seamus had just drawn two men, one small and fat, the other tall and thin, looking exactly like Laurel and Hardy.

She couldn't believe her eyes. "That's Shavitov and Lerntowski!" she gasped. "But they're dead! We saw them die!"

2
Florence Phones Home

Seamus didn't reply.

"You know they're dead," Aisling repeated. "They were on the *Fafnir* when it was torpedoed in Iceland last summer. They must have been burnt to death." She shuddered at the memory of that night in Iceland when they'd watched the Viking ship, with Shavitov, Lerntowski and another S.K.U.N.K. agent on board, sink in a blaze of flames.

"Don't count on it." Seamus smiled grimly. "These two unsavoury gentlemen have as many lives as that overfed moggy there."

Mulligan stretched, opened one eye and then went back to sleep again.

Aisling stared at her godfather. "They must be dead! And anyway, even if they aren't, what on earth would they be doing at Greenham Common? That's an American nuclear aircraft base."

"It is indeed. Your general knowledge never ceases to astound me."

Aisling ignored his sarcasm. "Well, what would they want there?" she repeated.

"A McDonald's hamburger and French fries, perhaps?"

"Be serious."

"I am serious. I am also hungry. Why don't you exercise your amazing culinary skills and heat up something from the freezer instead of hanging around here annoying me?"

Aisling thought of reminding him that it had been his idea that she should come all the way up to the attic in the first place. She decided not to—it wasn't worth the hassle. She wondered if she had the nerve to dish him up one of Mulligan's tins of cat food with some frozen vegetables and pretend it was stew. If she put enough garlic into it...

"Well? What are you hanging about for?" Seamus demanded. "It's nearly lunchtime. Go and make me something to eat."

"You still haven't told me why you've painted Shavitov and Lerntowski into that picture." Aisling looked at the canvas again. She pointed to the makeshift tents. "Is that what protesters live in at Greenham Common? I can't imagine Florence living in one of those." She thought of the way Florence kept house for Seamus and Archie: living in a tent seemed the last thing she would enjoy.

"Greenham Common, Greenham Common," Seamus mimicked. "Are you blind as well as stupid, child? Does that look like an airforce base?"

Aisling paid more attention to the buildings in the background of the painting. "No. Now you come to mention it. It's more like...I don't know...a nuclear reactor or something."

"Ten out of ten. Go to the top of the class. Or, even better, go downstairs and make my lunch and leave me in peace. Out!"

"Where is Florence then? Is that Sellafield? Or

Chernobyl? What's she doing there?"

"Probably at this moment she's doing what you should be doing: cooking. Now, for the last time, get out." Seamus picked up his brush and stared gloomily at the canvas, ignoring her completely.

Aisling decided she might as well leave; she wouldn't get anything more out of him now. She slammed the door behind her. If it annoyed him, so much the better. He was impossible. She'd proved to him twice, now, that she wasn't just a stupid little schoolgirl. She'd even saved his life the last time they'd gone after S.K.U.N.K.. But it made no difference to him. He still treated her like a baby.

She stamped downstairs to the kitchen and opened the freezer. Dozens of foilwrapped packages, all neatly labelled, stared up at her. She shut her eyes, went "eenie-meenie-minie-mo" with her finger and stabbed down at one of the packages. She opened her eyes and lifted it out. "Osso Bucco" the label said. It would have to do.

She removed the foil, plonked the dish in the microwave and set the programme to defrost and reheat. Maybe there was some rat poison in the garden shed? Would Seamus notice the taste in Osso Bucco, whatever that was? She imagined the headline in the *Irish Times*: *Elderly Irish artist found dead in Dalkey house. Schoolgirl helping the police with their enquiries.*

There was a ping. She looked at the microwave. It wasn't even halfway through its programme. The kitchen phone sat on the shelf above it: was that what had pinged? Very carefully, Aisling eased the receiver off its rest.

She heard Florence speaking to Seamus on the attic

extension. "Are you sure Aisling's feeding you all right? And is she eating properly herself? She's a growing child, you know."

"We're both fine." Seamus cut his sister short. "What took you so long to get in touch? Too busy gossiping with all those other females, no doubt, to bother about an abandoned old cripple."

"You are not abandoned. Aisling and her mother are looking after you, better than you deserve, I'm quite sure."

"Hmph. Anyway, it's as well you finally got around to ringing me. John Smith called yesterday and he seems to think S.K.U.N.K. is back in business and is taking an interest in nuclear waste. Have you noticed anything suspicious over there?"

"No." Florence sounded thoughtful. "There's quite a bit of nuclear waste being stockpiled at Sellafield now, waiting for the new THORP processing plant to start up. It's not only British waste: ships are coming in and out regularly to Barrow-in-Furness, bringing waste from abroad to be reprocessed here. We're trying to make people see how dangerous THORP is. And we're also trying to stop the shipments getting in. I'm going down to Barrow myself now, to help with manning the picket line, so it might be a little longer before I come home."

"What do you mean, a little longer?" Seamus exploded. "The agreement was that you had a week over there. Not the rest of your life. You are due back home on Saturday, and don't you forget it. Your husband may be away gallivanting around the world, but I need you here."

Aisling waited curiously to hear how Florence would answer. She had never understood why Florence allowed

11

herself to be bullied by Seamus; anyone of her own generation would have left him years ago. She wondered if Florence would defy him now.

"I may stay on for a couple of extra days," Florence said firmly. "And I certainly intend to come back here on a regular basis to help the others with the picket. Both you and Archie can manage quite well without me and you know it."

"Archie's always off on a boat somewhere. And I need you." Seamus sounded like a spoiled baby, Aisling thought. "Aisling and her mother aren't the same."

"I'm sure they aren't. And I hope you're being more polite to them than you are to me and expressing your gratitude now and again. You know they don't have to give so much time to you."

"Hmph."

"Anyhow. I intend to go down to Barrow with a few of the girls—"

"The girls? What are you, part of the front row of a chorus line?"

Aisling grinned. Florence continued as if Seamus hadn't interrupted her. "—to see if we can persuade the crew of the next spent-nuclear-fuel carrier from Italy to take their dangerous waste elsewhere. I shall stay there over the weekend and probably be back on Monday or Tuesday. I hope you haven't forgotten that Hermann Souter's son Peter is arriving in Dublin today and that he's going to stay with us for a holiday while his father's at that scientific conference in Outer Mongolia?"

Seamus was silent.

"I thought as much. You really are the most self-centred old man."

Aisling giggled out loud. She quickly put her hand over the telephone mouthpiece, but it was too late.

"So that's what you do instead of making my lunch, is it?" Seamus shouted down the phone. "Eavesdropping! This, for your information, is a private conversation: if we'd wanted it broadcast to the nation we'd have used a loudspeaker."

"Good morning, Aisling." Florence sounded quite unperturbed. "How are you coping? I hope Seamus is behaving himself."

"Behaving myself! Me? Behaving myself?" Seamus spluttered.

Aisling ignored him. "I'm fine, Florence," she answered sweetly. "And he's really no trouble at all. Are you enjoying protesting? And is Peter really coming here today?"

"Protesting is cold and wet and uncomfortable and enjoying is not a word I'd use to describe it, but I am certainly glad I came. As for Peter, he should be arriving from Switzerland this afternoon. I've made up the spare bed for him in the back room. Perhaps you'd put a hot water bottle in it to make sure it's properly aired and..."

"May I remind you that this is a reversed charges phonecall in prime time at the most expensive rate," Seamus interrupted. "If the two of you have quite finished making your domestic arrangements—I obviously have no say in who stays here or for how long; I sometimes wonder if I own this house or if it's just a hotel—I'd be grateful if you would stop supporting Telecom Éireann and ring off."

"I'm glad to hear you're still yourself, Seamus," Florence said calmly, "and not pining for me. Give Peter my love when he arrives. And look after him, Aisling, please. Remember, boys need a lot to eat."

"Hmph," Seamus growled.

Aisling bit back a retort about sexual equality: Florence was too old to change now. "I will, Florence," she promised. "See you."

"Bye." Florence put down the phone.

"Are you still there, big ears?" Seamus sounded gruff.

Yes, Noddy, Aisling mouthed.

"What's happened to my lunch?"

Aisling glanced at the microwave. "It's ready. I'll send it up right away."

She took the package out of the microwave and divided its contents between two plates. It smelt fantastic, but then, most of Florence's meals did. One thing about this week, she thought, she was certainly trying out new dishes. She put a finger into the stew and licked it. She imagined herself writing the "Table for Two" column in the *Irish Times*: *The Osso Bucco was smothered in a thick creamy sauce and rich with an aroma of herbs and wine...*

The doorbell rang.

She wiped her finger on a tea towel and went to answer it. With a bit of luck, it might be John Smith. At least he would be more willing to tell her what was going on. Then another thought struck her: if Seamus was right and Shavitov and Lerntowski were still alive, it might be one of them! She stopped short, halfway across the hall. The doorbell rang again.

She gave herself a shake. Seamus going on about S.K.U.N.K. again was making her neurotic: she knew the two men were dead. And yet...

Telling herself that she was being stupid, she ignored the bell and went up to the parlour on the first floor. She felt sick. Just the thought of Shavitov made her skin crawl as her hair tried to stand on end. He and Lerntowski *had* to be dead.

The parlour smelt musty. Its dark velvet curtains had been drawn to shield the furniture from the sunlight. As the bell rang for a third time, Aisling felt her way round heavy armchairs and fragile tables to the window. Very carefully, she pulled back a corner of the curtain and looked down to the doorstep beneath.

She let out her breath in an audible sigh. A large person dressed in a navy raincoat stood in front of the door, but it wasn't Shavitov—unless he was wearing a headscarf and had grown a massive bosom in the meantime. She raced downstairs and opened the door.

The woman on the doorstep held out a hand. "Antonia Browne," she announced. "With an 'e.' I hope I didn't disturb you."

3

Miss Antonia Browne

T he stranger reminded Aisling of a badly-wrapped parcel: her headscarf was slipping to release untidy strands of straggly mouse-brown hair and the tightly-fastened belt of her coat divided her body into two formless bulges. Her face, as soft and squelchy as a marshmallow, was smeared with lipstick and luminous blue eye-shadow and her smile, Aisling thought, looked as if it had been stuck on like a stamp.

The woman consulted a small red notebook. "Is this Seamus O'Toole's residence, love?"

Aisling hated being called "love." "Yes," she said coldly. "What do you want?"

The woman looked pained. She smiled again, as falsely as before. "I'm here from St Philomena's Society for the Aged and Infirm. I gather your grandaddy is both. Will you show me in to him, please, chicken?"

"Chicken" was even worse than "love." And "grandaddy" was for babies. "My godfather is working," Aisling said even more coldly. "He doesn't like to be disturbed."

"Oh, I won't disturb him." The woman picked up her bag and pushed past Aisling into the hall. "Where is he then? In here?" She waddled through to the kitchen. "Oh

16

dear! Down, pussy! Bad pussy! Pussy shouldn't be on the table! Bad, bad pussy!"

Aisling leant up against the door jamb and watched the fat woman wave her notebook at Mulligan, who was on top of the table, crouched defensively over a plate which still showed a few traces of Osso Bucco. (The other plate, she noticed, had already been cleaned to a standard of which Florence would have been proud.) Aisling grinned as she looked at him: his tail was lashing, his ears were flat, his eyes were big and black and he was growling like a smallish orange police dog faced with a particularly nasty burglar.

"I think you'd better leave him," she said helpfully. "If he goes for you, he might rip out your eyes."

The woman stopped waving her notebook and stepped back. Mulligan gave her one last look and returned to licking the second plate clean.

The woman tried a rather sickly smile. "Where did you say Mr O'Toole was then, pet?"

Aisling looked at the two empty plates. She'd have to defrost something else now and Seamus would be livid at being kept waiting so long for his lunch. She knew he'd be even madder if she let the woman up to the studio, but the thought of what he would say to someone sent specially by St Philomena's Society for the Aged and Infirm to help him was too tempting to miss. And if they stayed arguing for long enough, she'd have time to come back down again and get something else out of the freezer and heat it up. "His studio's at the top of the stairs," she said. "I'll show you up."

She waited outside the studio door for the woman to

17

catch up with her (Miss Browne obviously didn't go in for fitness training: she was practically crawling up the last flight of stairs and panting like a St Bernard in a heat-wave). Then she opened the attic door, stood back and let Miss Browne go in. As she'd hoped, Seamus's face made the climb up to the attic worthwhile. "What in the name of little green leprechauns are you doing bursting into my studio, woman?"

The woman took a deep breath, steadied herself and smiled bravely once again. "I'm Antonia Browne. With an 'e'..." she started to explain.

"I don't care if you're Antonia Browne with a face-lift! I asked you what you were doing invading my privacy like this. Just when I should be having my lunch!"

Aisling hastily ducked out of the room.

"And don't think I didn't see you there, Aisling. Come here and explain yourself. I have been waiting for exactly twenty-two minutes for you to bring up some food (hardly a feat of astonishing ingenuity, considering how much preparation you have to put into a frozen meal), and instead of bringing me some boeuf bourguignon or chilli con carne or whatever, you bring me an overweight woman who looks as if she's going to have a heart attack and who tells me her name is Antonia Browne. With an 'e.' "

Miss Browne stepped up to the bed and patted Seamus's arm. "There, there, now. Don't upset yourself, pet. You know, at your age, it doesn't do to get upset. And don't worry about your meal. Just give me a minute to get my breath back and I'll go down and cook you some nice scrambled eggs."

Seamus pulled his arm away as if it had been burned. "Upset myself?" he spluttered. "Scrambled eggs! Why, you…you…"

She took advantage of his speechlessness. "I'm from St Philomena's Society for the…St Philomena's Society," she said firmly. "We've heard that dear Florence is away so I've been asked to come and look after you. You don't need to worry any more. I can stay as long as you need me."

Seamus looked as if he was going to burst. Then he clamped his mouth tight shut and, Aisling thought, must have counted to ten because when he finally spoke he sounded quite reasonable. "Fine. Good," he said. "Since I don't need you at all, you can go now. Goodbye. Aisling will show you out."

Miss Browne smiled warmly at him. She wagged a fat finger. "It's nice to see you so playful, pet. As Mummy used to say, God rest her, it doesn't do to get downhearted. Now you just lie back there and rest and I'll have your dinner up in two shakes of a lamb's tail."

"Come back here, woman!" Seamus yelled. But Miss Browne was already bouncing down the stairs. He turned to Aisling. "Get her out of my house!"

"How?" Aisling saw herself shoving Miss Browne out through the front door like a removals man pushing a grand piano. Or like a mouse pushing a very large elephant. She didn't have much faith in the outcome.

"I don't know. You let her in; you get her out. And then bring me up my lunch. A man could starve to death in this madhouse."

Aisling trudged downstairs. As she reached the ground

floor, she heard the sound of banging from the kitchen, punctuated by hisses and yowls from Mulligan. She rushed into the kitchen just as Miss Browne slammed the outside door and leant a broom up against it. "That's better."

"What have you done to Mulligan?" Aisling ran to the door to let him back in, but Miss Browne got there first. She turned the key and removed it. "Now, now, chicken. He'll have to learn that cats aren't allowed into the house. Why don't you find me a tray and set it while I scramble up some nice eggs for your grandad."

"He's not my grandad, he's my godfather. I told you that before. And he told me to get rid...to show you out."

Miss Browne smiled again. "He has a marvellous sense of humour for such an old man, I'll give him that, dearie. Now, you just fetch that tray. I take it the eggs are in here?" She opened the fridge door.

"Did you hear me? Seamus doesn't want you here. You're to go!"

The woman ignored her. She took four eggs from the fridge, broke them into a bowl, added half a carton of milk and salt and pepper and started to mix them with a fork. "I'm going to ring the police," Aisling threatened.

"I wouldn't bother, pet. They know the good work St Philomena's do. And they know your grandaddy is all on his own and needing help. But, if you want to call up Paddy Flynn at the garda station (Sergeant Flynn to you, chick), by all means do so. Sure, why don't you just give him a ring there now and tell him his Aunt Antonia wants to speak to him? It's a long time since I've had a proper chat with little Pádraig."

Aisling's hand had been hovering over the phone. She let it drop. If this ghastly woman was related to the garda sergeant, then he certainly wouldn't tell her to clear off. Especially if she'd been sent by the church to look after Seamus.

She grinned suddenly. Maybe this was just what Seamus needed. It was about time someone bossed him about for a change—and if anyone was capable of it, Antonia Browne was that person. On top of which, if St Philomena's Society were looking after Seamus, then she needn't bother any more. An even pleasanter thought struck her: there would probably be a bus down to Athlone this afternoon. If she caught it, she'd still manage to get a couple of days on the Shannon with Louise and her family. "Fine," she said happily. "In that case, I'll leave him to you."

4

St Philomena's Society

When Aisling got home, her parents were drinking coffee in the front room. Mrs Daly looked up.

"Don't tell me you've forgotten something again, Aisling. Or are you just looking for an excuse to get away from Seamus for a while? I know he's not the easiest person in the world to get on with, but it's only for one week..."

Aisling flung herself on to the sofa and kicked off her shoes. "It's over, finished, finito, the end," she announced. "Seamus has found himself a full-time babysitter and I've been made redundant."

Mr Daly looked at her suspiciously. "What do you mean, a full-time babysitter?"

"St Philomena's Society For Looking After Selfish Bad-tempered Old Men has taken over. In the shape of one Miss Antonia Browne, with an 'e,' who doesn't like cats and who is staying there till Florence comes back."

"Who?"

"I told you. St Philomena's Society. It must be something to do with the church. Anyway, it lets us off the hook. Can I go to Athlone now?"

"I've never heard of them." Mrs Daly looked puzzled.

"Are you sure you got the name right?"

"It was something like that, anyway. The sort of do-gooding charity group that would send some interfering old cow like Miss Antonia Browne to boss people about."

"That's no way to talk about anyone, Aisling. And especially someone who is acting in Christian charity." Mrs Daly frowned and finished her coffee. "I suppose I'd better go up and have a word with her just to see what exactly the arrangements are. It'd be too much to hope that this woman, whatever her name is, will be doing the nights too."

Aisling remembered the bag Miss Browne had dumped in the hall. "I think she intends to move in permanently. She certainly had a big enough bag with her."

"Well, I can't deny that that would be a relief. It'd be nice to sleep in my own bed again, for a change. Perhaps you could run me up there, Frank, on your way back to work?"

"What about Athlone, then?" Aisling shrieked as her parents left the room.

Mrs Daly poked her head back round the door. "Athlone?"

"Can I go down to Athlone this afternoon? Louise and her family will still be there."

"Well, I suppose…if you're sure Seamus doesn't need you. You'd better wait till I speak to this woman, though, just in case there's been a mistake. Why don't you give Louise a ring and check that it's okay with her parents? Bye."

The front door slammed. Rats, Aisling thought. If she starts nattering to Miss Browne, she'll probably be there all afternoon and I'll miss the bus. "Double rats," she said out loud. "Double, triple and quadruple rats!" She had suddenly remembered that Louise, being on a boat, didn't have a phone. What a miserable Easter holiday this had turned out to be.

With a sigh, she put her feet up on the sofa and turned on the TV.

□

Ten minutes later the doorbell rang. She decided to ignore it. Her brother Kevin could answer it. She was fed up.

Then the door opened behind her. *"Grüssti*, Ash! *Wie geht's*? How are you?"

She whirled round. "Peter! I'd completely forgotten about you!"

"Thanks. That's the second really warm welcome I've had this afternoon." He wasn't joking, Aisling realised: he looked upset.

"Come on, Peter. You know I didn't mean it that way. When Seamus told me this morning that you were coming, it was fantastic. Honest. And it's great to see you again. I mean it."

Peter smiled at last. "I'm sorry, Ash. It's just that when I found out that Seamus didn't want to see me and then you said you'd forgotten all about me, well…"

"What do you mean, Seamus didn't want to see you? Florence rang this morning and reminded him you were coming. I was to warm your bed and everything. Oops, I forgot about that, too."

Peter grinned. "I'm sure I'll survive without a warmed

24

bed. It's much colder in Switzerland than here, anyway. But it doesn't look as if I'm going to have a bed at all."

"Did Seamus tell you that? Don't mind him. He was probably in a bad mood because of that new housekeeper woman he has. You know Seamus, he gets grumpy for the sake of being grumpy. He doesn't mean it."

"Is that who that woman was? His new housekeeper?"

"Yes. She's quite something, isn't she? I'd love to be a fly on the wall when she really starts bossing him around." Aisling grinned at the thought.

Peter didn't smile. "She wouldn't even let me see Seamus. She said he had asked her to tell me to go away, that there was no room there for me, that there had been a mistake."

"That's funny. But maybe she just didn't want to bother Seamus and never even told him you'd arrived. It's okay, though: Mum's up there now. I'll just ring up and tell her what's happened and she can sort it out with Seamus." A thought struck her. "Or would you like me to ask her if you can stay here instead? It'd be a heck of a lot better than you having to live with Seamus and Miss Antonia Browne, with or without an 'e.' "

Peter cheered up. "*Das wäre prima!* Would your mother mind? I didn't like that woman—what did you call her—at all."

"Miss Antonia Browne. Hold on a minute while I ring Mum."

Aisling dialled Seamus's number.

To her surprise, Miss Browne answered the phone. "Seamus O'Toole's residence. Can I help you?" She sounded as smarmy as ever.

25

"Er...This is Aisling here. Would you put the phone through to Seamus, please."

"Seamus is resting at the moment. I'm afraid he can't speak to you now, chicken."

"He won't mind," Aisling said stubbornly. "Just put the phone through to the studio."

"I told you he's resting. And even if he weren't, I am certainly not going to go up all these stairs with a message. Why don't you ring back later, pet?"

"But he has a phone in his studio!" Aisling couldn't understand what was happening. Seamus always had the phone right beside his bed. Why hadn't he answered it himself?

"There is no phone in his studio. If you want to give him a message, just tell me and I'll let him know as soon as he wakes up. Don't take all day, now, chicken. I've a lot of things to do."

"But..." What on earth was going on? How could there be no phone in the studio when there had always been a phone in the studio and Florence had been talking to him on that phone only a few hours before? Aisling decided to try another tack. "Can I speak to my mother then, please?"

"Your mother, pet?"

It was like banging your head against a padded wall. "Yes," Aisling said through gritted teeth. "My mother. She was on her way up to see you. She must be there by now."

"Oh your mother's been and gone, chick. She should be home any minute, so I wouldn't worry, dearie, if I were you. Cheery-bye now."

26

"Hey, wait a minute!" Aisling yelled. But the phone was dead.

"What was all that about?" Peter asked.

Aisling frowned. "I don't know. There's something very strange going on. She wouldn't let me speak to Seamus at all."

"Did she give any reason?"

"She said he was resting. Seamus never rests."

"He's getting old," Peter pointed out. "Old people often rest."

"Not Seamus. And even if he was resting, that still doesn't explain why he didn't answer the phone; it's right beside his bed, after all. The cow said she was downstairs, so she must have been answering from the kitchen extension. Why didn't it ring in the studio?"

"Maybe he was asleep and didn't hear it?"

"She actually said that there was no phone in the studio. Why should she say that?"

"I don't know," Peter said soothingly. "But your mother should be back soon. Why don't you ask her?"

□

Mrs Daly wasn't much help, however.

"Did you see Seamus?" Aisling asked eagerly as soon as she came home. "What's happening up there? Why didn't he answer the phone?"

"I didn't see him. Miss Browne said he was resting, so I didn't want to disturb him."

Aisling looked at Peter. He shrugged his shoulders. "So?"

27

"Why didn't you insist on seeing him?" Aisling asked. "How do you know he was all right? She might have done something to him."

"Who might have done what? Do you mean Miss Browne might have done something to Seamus?" Mrs Daly sighed. "What on earth are you imagining now, Aisling?"

"We don't know who she is. And she was horrid to Mulligan. For all we know, she might be..." Aisling broke off. "Did you check her papers or anything?"

"No, I did not. And I didn't take her fingerprints either. Really, Aisling, you must stop letting your imagination run away with you. Miss Browne seems a very capable, caring person and we are very lucky that St Philomena's should have sent someone round to look after Seamus for us. I was very impressed with her, I must say."

"Did you at least check that she is what she says she is? I mean, do you know if there really is a St Philomena's Society? And that they have a Miss Browne working for them?"

"Of course she's genuine. Why wouldn't she be?" Mrs Daly spoke shortly.

"Don't you think you should check? I mean, there are all these cases of granny-bashing nowadays, one should never be too careful."

"Seamus is not what anyone would call a granny," Peter pointed out with a grin.

Aisling glared at him. She'd have thought he at least would have agreed that there was something fishy going on. But instead of helping her explain to her mother, he was only making things worse.

"Sorry, Ash." Peter looked suitably contrite. "But I agree with your mother. I didn't like this woman either, but there is no reason to suppose she is anything other than what she says she is. Why would she pretend to be something she is not?"

"I don't know," Aisling admitted. But I definitely mean to find out, she added to herself.

"Would you like to come out for a walk?" she asked Peter politely.

5
John Smith Takes a Hand

isling led Peter to Dalkey. As they passed the church, she turned in through the gates to the presbytery.

"Why are you calling here?" Peter asked. "I thought we were going for a walk."

"We were. And now we've arrived."

"I'm sorry?"

"I'm going to ask the priest if he's heard of St Philomena's Society. If he hasn't, then we'll know Miss Browne's a fake."

Aisling rang the bell.

The door was opened by a middle-aged lady wearing an apron. She peeled off a pair of yellow rubber gloves. "I'm sorry, kids. Father Quinn is out at the moment. Can I take a message?"

Aisling hesitated. "Well...maybe you could help us. Do you know anything about St Philomena's Society for the old and sick?"

The housekeeper beamed. "St Philomena's Society for the Aged and Infirm? Of course. I'm a member of it myself. Have you an old or infirm relative you would like us to look after?"

Aisling looked at her closely. Was she telling the truth,

or was she just a good actress?

She tried again. "You wouldn't happen to have a member called Antonia Browne, would you? With an 'e'?"

"Antonia? Yes, of course. She's one of our best volunteers. Did you want Antonia particularly? I'm sorry, but she actually has a client at the moment. Perhaps next week?"

Aisling frowned. It all sounded so plausible, and yet…"That's all right. Thank you very much."

Peter took hold of her arm. "Come on, Ash. We have to be going."

"Are you sure, dear? I mean, if you'd like anyone else to help you, we have lots of members."

"No, thank you," Peter repeated. "Thanks very much. Goodbye."

He dragged Aisling away. "There. Now are you satisfied? She is just what she said she was."

"We still don't know that," Aisling insisted as they walked down Castle Street together. "I mean, how do we even know that woman was Father Quinn's housekeeper? If Antonia Browne is working for S.K.U.N.K., they would probably have guessed that someone would check up here. That woman could be working for S.K.U.N.K. as well!"

"I thought you thought St Philomena's was a gang of—how did you put it—granny-bashers? Where does S.K.U.N.K. come into it?"

"That was just for Mum's benefit. I've suspected Antonia Browne of belonging to S.K.U.N.K. for ages."

"But S.K.U.N.K.'s finished!" Peter said in surprise. "My father told me that Shavitov and Lerntowski were killed in Iceland last year. Why on earth should you suddenly think of them now?"

Aisling explained about Seamus's painting and told him about the conversation she'd had with her godfather that morning. "And if John Smith thinks S.K.U.N.K. is causing trouble again, they could easily be here," she finished. "I mean, they must want to get even with Seamus. If this Antonia Browne woman isn't a S.K.U.N.K. agent, if she is what she says she is, why won't she let anyone talk to Seamus, even on the phone?"

"It does sound a bit suspicious," Peter admitted. "And I hadn't realised John Smith was involved. Maybe you're right." He grinned suddenly: "Though I still can't see S.K.U.N.K. planting housekeepers all over Ireland just to get even with Seamus. What do you suggest we do?"

"We could try to sneak up and talk to Seamus without her knowing."

Peter frowned. "Perhaps. But I think we should see John Smith first. If that woman is part of S.K.U.N.K., maybe we should ask him to come up to Seamus's house with us."

Aisling hesitated. She was really worried about Seamus. But John Smith had once worked for MI5 and still kept in touch with both the British and the Irish Secret Services and he'd been a fantastic help the past couple of times they'd tangled with S.K.U.N.K. Maybe Peter was right; if they were going to have to face S.K.U.N.K. up in Seamus's house, he'd be a good man to have on their side. "Okay," she agreed. "Only hurry up. Seamus is a grouchy old horror who drives me up the wall, but I'd hate to see him murdered all the same."

Fortunately John Smith's bookshop in Dalkey wasn't

far away. When they got there, they found it deserted. There was no sign of John Smith and not a single customer.

"He's been kidnapped!" Aisling whispered as the bell over the door gave a last sof t tinkle and silence settled like dust around them again. "S.K.U.N.K. must have got here first!"

"He's probably just gone out for a cup of coffee or something." But Peter sounded worried too.

"He'd have locked the door if he'd gone out."

A cough came from behind the frosted glass partition which separated the office from the rest of the shop. Aisling jumped. "There's somebody in there!"

A figure moved behind the frosted glass. Aisling grabbed Peter's arm. Then a balding head poked round the door. It was followed by a rather stout body dressed in a pair of crumpled corduroy trousers and a shabby tweed jacket.

"Aisling! To what do I owe this honour? And Peter Souter, all the way from Switzerland! How is your father, Peter, not to mention all those Cs: cantons, conglomerates, corporations, companies, chocolates, cheeses, cuckoo clocks, chemicals...? Sometimes I wonder why Switzerland doesn't file itself under C completely and call itself Citzerland or something. That way it would all get into one volume of the encyclopedia." John Smith had once pretended to be an encyclopedia salesman and he never let anyone forget it.

"We thought you'd been..." Aisling had been going to say "kidnapped" but it sounded stupid now that he was standing in front of them.

"Yes?"

"Nothing."

"Aha! So you thought I'd been nothinged. I must look that up in the encyclopedia some time. It sounds painful."

John Smith might have been a great help in the past, Aisling reminded herself, but he was also a pain in the backside. She scowled at him.

"Aisling's worried about Seamus," Peter explained quickly.

"Oh dear." John Smith looked sympathetic. "What's he done now? Refused to eat one of your culinary (from the Latin *culina*, a kitchen, hence meaning to do with cooking, as I'm sure you'll be delighted to know, Aisling) masterpieces in the form of a reheated cold dinner?"

"He's being held prisoner," Aisling said stiffly.

"Seamus? Held prisoner?" John Smith dropped his bantering tone. "Where? By whom?"

"In his own house. By S.K.U.N.K."

"Really? I didn't think they'd act so fast. Or that they'd bother old Seamus this time. For once he's not involved, as far as I know."

Aisling looked smugly at Peter. "I told you it was S.K.U.N.K."

"Told him what? Oh. You mean you *don't* know that Seamus is being held by S.K.U.N.K.? Forgive my sceptical mind, but do you know if he's being held at all? Or is this just a figment of your imagination?"

"I wish people would shut up about my imagination. Seamus is a prisoner in his own house; for all you know he's been poisoned or shot or thrown down the stairs or anything, just because you won't take me seriously and do something about it."

John Smith looked at her steadily for a minute. "Okay," he said finally. "I'll take you seriously. You think S.K.U.N.K. have taken over Seamus's house. But if they have, my impetuous young friends, you must admit that there's no point in just rushing up there. We have to decide on a plan of action. For example, do we bring in the forces of law and order, otherwise known as Sergeant Flynn and his merry men, or do we deal with this one ourselves? How many of them are there?"

"Er...one." Aisling was embarrassed.

"Well, that's a relief. Who is it? Shavitov? Lerntowski? Is he armed?"

"They're both dead, aren't they?" Peter said. "I thought they were killed in Iceland."

"The devil looks after his own," John Smith said gravely. Is it Shavitov, Aisling?"

"Well, no. It's a woman. A Miss Antonia Browne. With an 'e.' "

John Smith's mouth twitched at the corners. "Are you telling me Seamus is being held prisoner by one single solitary woman?"

"Yes." Aisling felt more and more of a fool.

"In that case, what are we waiting for? Let's get up there and beard this Amazon in her den. You *do* know who the Amazons were, don't you? Or shall I bring an encyclopedia with us so you can look it up in the car?"

"I don't care who the Amazons were," Aisling muttered. "Let's get on with it."

"God spare me from the younger generation. Not only do you have closed minds but you are proud of it," John

Smith complained as he ushered them out of the shop and locked the door behind them. "The Amazons were, according to Greek legend, a tribe of women fiercer than any men. I'd have thought you'd have been interested in them as role models, Aisling."

"Huh."

"Do you drive this?" Peter gazed in awe at the sleek black Alpha Romeo sports car.

"Indeed I do. Drive, steer, pilot, chauffeur: whichever you prefer. Hop in, both of you, and we'll away and rescue Seamus from the dragon. Though I must admit," he added as they turned left and roared up the hill towards Seamus's house, "I find it stretches my imagination to the ultimate (from the Latin *ultimus*, the furthest, Aisling) to see Seamus in the role of a fair damsel in distress."

□

Aisling wanted to try to get in by a back window, but John Smith insisted on ringing the door bell first. "If your Miss Browne is a S.K.U.N.K. agent," he said reasonably, "she won't let us see him and then we can think of attempting burglary. But if she isn't, then we'll have saved ourselves a possible charge of breaking and entering and I'm getting a bit long in the tooth to be convicted of a felony (otherwise known as a crime, Aisli...) Ah, good afternoon, Madam." Miss Browne had just opened the door. John Smith smiled at her delightedly. "Do I have the pleasure of addressing Miss Antonia Browne? With, I believe, an 'e'?"

Miss Browne blushed. "I'm afraid you have the

advantage over me, dearie."

John Smith bowed, practically clicking his heels together: if he'd been wearing a hat, he'd have taken it off, Aisling thought in disgust. "I do beg your pardon. John Aloysius Smith, at your service."

Miss Browne simpered. Aisling stifled a giggle: Aloysius!

"I'm most dreadfully sorry to disturb you, but myself and young Aisling here (and Peter, whom I gather you've met) would like a word with Seamus. Shall we go up?"

To Aisling's surprise, Miss Browne stood aside. "He'll be delighted to see you, Mr Smith. He's had a good rest this afternoon and a bit of company will do him a power of good. I'll make you a pot of tea, so, and bring it up to you in a minute."

"Thank you kindly, ma'am. That's just what the doctor ordered." And John Smith led them into the house.

"It's a trick," whispered Aisling as she panted up the stairs behind him. (John Smith moved very fast for someone as unfit as he looked.) "Be careful at the top: they may be waiting in the attic."

He ignored her and opened the studio door.

Seamus, who was sitting up in bed, pushed his hand quickly under the duvet. He reminded Aisling of a little boy who's been caught doing something naughty.

"What in the name of Beelzebub are you all doing, barging in here without so much as a by-your-leave?" he roared. "This isn't a stately home! I don't have an open-to-the-public day! Will you all get out and leave me alone!"

The whistle went on the speaking tube from the kitchen. Seamus patted his short grey hair and reached

for the mouthpiece above his bed. "Antonia? What can I
do for you?"

Aisling had never heard him sounding so polite.

Miss Browne's voice boomed over the intercom. "I've
made a nice pot of tea for you, pet," she said. "It's coming
up now. Don't let these visitors tire you out."

"Thank you very much indeed. It is really most kind
of you. You shouldn't have gone to such trouble." Seamus
was almost stuttering in his desire to please. He replaced
the speaking tube on its hook and beamed into space.
Aisling tried very hard to keep a straight face.

Seamus looked at her. "What are you grinning like a
drunken baboon for?" he growled in his customary voice.
"Get the tea out of the hatch and make yourself useful
for a change."

He pressed a button beside his bed and a panel in the
wall opened. Ropes moved in the shaft behind it and a
platform, bearing a laden tray, came slowly up from the
kitchen to the level of the studio. Aisling brought the
tray over to Seamus's bed. Instead of Florence's lace tray-
cloth and china cups, there were four kitchen mugs and
a big delft teapot on the bare tray, together with a ghastly-
looking shop cake covered in sticky pink icing.

"Good," Seamus said. "Just what the doctor ordered.
I suggest you be mother, Aisling, while someone tells me
to what I owe the honour of this visit."

"Peter is supposed to be staying here and she sent
him away and Mum wasn't allowed up to see you either
and you haven't even said hello to Peter now he's here..."

"Will you pour that tea, child. Hello, Peter, if that
makes you any happier. And cut me a piece of that cake;

it looks delicious."

Aisling almost exploded. "You really are the rudest person I've ever met!"

Seamus turned his full attention to Peter. "Good afternoon, Peter. I trust you had a good journey. Aisling will show you to your room in a minute. I hope you will be very happy here." He turned back to Aisling. "Now can I have my tea?"

John Smith took the teapot from her before she could empty it over her godfather. "Allow me," he said. "We've come to ask you about S.K.U.N.K.," he explained as he deftly poured four mugs of tea and cut the cake into slices. "Aisling thinks your Miss Browne is a member of that breathtaking bunch of blackguards."

"She would. Despite being my godchild, she bears a certain resemblance to Winnie the Pooh, who was, if you remember, a bear of very little brain."

Aisling wasn't listening. She was staring at the skylight. "Did you hear that?"

"What?" the others said in unison.

"Shh." Aisling listened again. "It's a cat. On the roof. It must be Mulligan!"

She jumped up, nearly upsetting the teatray, raced to the console beside Seamus's bed and pressed one switch after another. The "teasmade" machine started to shriek, the light went on, the easel swayed across the bed, the radio blared...

"Will you stop that!" Seamus roared. He tried to push her hand away.

But Aisling continued to press the switches. Finally she found the one she wanted: the skylight swung open.

An orange head appeared in the gap. It gave a plaintive miaow.

"I knew it was Mulligan! Come on down, Mulligan. Poor Mulligan. Did that nasty lady lock you out?"

Mulligan leapt from the edge of the skylight with a delighted *prriau*. He landed heavily on Seamus's stomach. Seamus swore, swiped at him and the tray crashed to the floor. Tea spilled over the carpet and the pink cake skidded to a halt at the skirting board.

Mulligan leapt off the bed, rubbed himself quickly round Aisling's legs to show he was glad to see her again, and then attacked the cake like a one-cat swarm of locusts finding a field of juicy maize after two hundred miles of empty desert.

"Get that flying omnivore out of here!" Seamus was purple with rage. "First you disturb my rest and then you bombard me with monstrous felines and wreck my afternoon tea. Get out, all of you! Pick up that cat and GO!"

Aisling stared at the bed. The duvet had slipped when Seamus had thrown Mulligan off, and she could now see what Seamus had stuffed down under it when they'd arrived: a silver-backed hairbrush. They must have caught him just as he was brushing his hair. Seamus *brushing his hair*! It was unheard of.

She realised that John Smith was talking again. "So you're all right then, Seamus?" he was asking. "Miss Browne is a *bona fide* (don't bother checking the encyclopedia, Aisling: it's Latin for 'in good faith') Good Samaritan? You're not in any danger from S.K.U.N.K.?"

Seamus opened his mouth, changed his mind and shut

it again. He closed his eyes as if in pain. Then he took a deep breath and spoke very carefully and calmly, as if to a class of extremely stupid two-year-olds: "The only thing I am in danger from is flying cats. And people who are trying to raise my blood pressure by visiting me when I don't want visitors. I don't know where you got this crazy idea about Miss Browne from, but I promise you I am being looked after perfectly. Will that satisfy you or do you want it in writing? If not, get out."

John Smith smiled. "Just let me get this absolutely straight. Neither Shavitov nor Lerntowski has been bothering you and you are quite safe with Miss Browne. Though whether she is with you is another matter. Would you say that's a fair summing up of the situation? Just to put Aisling's mind at rest. She worries about you, you know."

Seamus took a deep breath. "For the last time: OUT!"

John Smith stood up. "I hope I'm not being unduly sensitive, but somehow I get the impression that your godfather would like to be alone for a while, Aisling. To commune with nature or something, no doubt. So come along now, both of you. Never let it be said that we outstayed our welcome."

"And take that blasted cat with you!" Seamus yelled, as Aisling reluctantly followed John Smith and Peter onto the landing.

She turned, pulled Mulligan away from the last few crumbs of cake and, without saying another word to Seamus, slung him over her shoulder and slammed the door behind her.

"Honest! Seamus gets worse and worse. I'm taking

Mulligan home with me: he's obviously half-starved here."

"Mulligan believes he's half-starved anywhere," John Smith commented. "But don't let that stop you."

"I won't," Aisling replied.

She handed Mulligan to Peter at the bottom of the stairs. "Hold him a minute while I get some tins of catfood."

She was just about to push the kitchen door open when she heard Seamus's voice at the other side of the door, booming through the speaking tube from the attic.

"I told you I'm sorry, Antonia. It was the fault of that blasted cat. I'd be really very grateful if you could send up another tray...Yes, I know it's a dreadful nuisance... No, I promise I won't make a habit of it..."

Aisling pushed the door open. Miss Browne put her hand across the mouthpiece of the speaking tube. "Are you going now, pet? Can you find your own way out?"

"Are you still there, Antonia?" Seamus bawled.

She took her hand off the mouthpiece. "There's no need to shout, chick," she said primly. "If you're really sorry for giving me all this extra work, I suppose I can make an exception, but it's just this once, you realise. Don't expect to be pampered like this all the time. I haven't got all day to be making cups of tea, or to be running up and down these stairs to clear up after you, you know."

"Yes, Antonia. I'm sorry. Thank you, Antonia."

Aisling grabbed a plastic bag, filled it with catfood tins from the cupboard and rushed out to join the others. "It's unbelievable!" she burst out as they got back into John Smith's car. "He lets her walk all over him! And he

was brushing his hair when we came into the studio! Did
you see the hairbrush? What on earth has she done to
him? She must have been giving him drugs."

John Smith grinned. "Maybe he's in love?"

"Don't be silly. She's obviously done something to him."

"He seemed all right to me," Peter objected. "Anyway,
once Florence comes home, Miss Browne will have to
leave. I think you're worrying about nothing."

"Ah yes, Florence. She's on holiday, is she, Aisling?"

"You have to be kidding. Archie's off with Thorwald
on the *Fafnir II*, following the Viking trade route to
Constantinople, so she's gone off herself to Sellafield to
demonstrate against recycling nuclear waste. Or rather,
to Barrow-in-Furness, wherever that is, according to what
she told Seamus. You'd think she was a student or
something, not an old woman. Obviously getting married
so late in life has affected her."

"Perhaps Florence cares about the future of the world,
Ash," Peter corrected her. "Not every middle-aged lady is
willing to sleep rough and risk being arrested for
something they believe in, you know. It is not something
to laugh about."

"Sorry. I only meant..."

"You mentioned Sellafield?" John Smith rescued her.
He swung the car round the one-way system into Hyde
Road. "And recycling nuclear waste. Now there's a
coincidence."

"What is?"

"I'm going over to England myself on this evening's
boat to inquire into the nuclear recycling business. It
might be a good idea for me to look Florence up."

"Can we come?" Aisling asked eagerly.

John Smith stopped the car outside her house. "Haven't you got a school to go to?"

"It's Easter. And my whole holiday's been ruined by having to babysit Seamus. And Peter's here too. It'd be much more interesting (and educational) for him to visit England as well as Ireland. And we wouldn't get in the way."

"Sorry. Not this time, folks. But I'll tell you what. If you're really worried about Peter's education, I'll leave you the keys to the shop. You know where the encyclopedias are kept. Feel free, both of you, to read up as much as you like about England or anything else that takes your fancy."

"Please!"

John Smith leant across her and opened the door. "Out! I promise to try to persuade Florence to come home with me tomorrow. Will that do you? With Florence here, as you so rightly pointed out, Seamus will have to behave himself. As things are, I'm not sure if it's entirely proper to have him and the incredible Miss Browne up there without a chaperone. And if you don't know what that is, look it up in a dictionary when you get in. I have a boat to catch."

"Rats," said Aisling as they watched the black car speed away. "Rats multiplied to the power of five hundred!"

6
Phonecalls

A isling and Peter went down to Dún Laoghaire harbour the next evening to meet the car ferry, but there was no sign of John Smith.

"He could have decided to stay on for a bit," Peter suggested.

Aisling grinned. "Maybe Florence has persuaded him to join the picket. Can't you just see him, marching up and down with a load of women chanting slogans?"

"Or lying in the mud in front of a transporter?"

"Maybe he's trying to sell them encyclopedias?"

"Seamus won't be pleased if Florence doesn't come back soon."

"I wouldn't bet on it," Aisling muttered. "The longer Florence stays away, the longer he can be all lovey-dovey with that Browne Cow woman. I don't know if she belongs to S.K.U.N.K. or not, but I do know I can't wait to see the back of her."

They were hardly home when the phone rang. Aisling picked up the receiver. Mulligan, assuming that they'd come back specially to feed him, jumped up onto the phone shelf and butted his nose into her face, purring like a vacuum cleaner. She pushed him away. "Leave me alone, you brute!"

"Is that any way to answer the telephone?" It was John Smith. "Lucky for you, I'm not unduly sensitive. Some people might take umbrage (originally from the Latin *umbra*, a shadow, but now meaning 'offence,' as I'm sure you're aware) if someone talked to them like that down the phone."

"Sorry. It was Mulligan. He's being a blasted nuisance."

Mulligan was now standing on her shoulders, poking his nose into her right ear. "Ah yes. I can hear him from here. Which is more than I can you. In the interests of cross-channel communication, I suggest you park him somewhere else; preferably at least three streets away. I shall while away the time admiring the graffiti in this phone box while you do so."

Aisling put down the phone, unhooked Mulligan from her jumper and dumped him roughly on Peter. "Open a tin of cat food for him, would you?" she hissed. "And then lock him in the kitchen. He's impossible." She went back to the phone. "Did you find out what you wanted?" she asked. "When are you coming back? Is Florence with you?"

"Not exactly." John Smith spoke quietly. "She seems to have disappeared."

"What?"

"Is that cat still whispering sweet nothings into your eardrum or have you gone deaf? Florence has disappeared."

"But where? How? When?"

"You sound like 'Twenty Questions.' Or was that before your generation?"

Aisling groaned. John Smith was worse than Seamus

at times. "What's happened to Florence? Is she in danger?"

"To be honest with you, I don't know. I asked at Sellafield and was told she'd gone down to Barrow-in-Furness with a whole group of protesters. There was a ship, the *Apocalypse* coming in from Italy carrying spent nuclear fuel rods and they were hoping to prevent it from docking. So I went along to Barrow myself to see what was going on."

"And?" Aisling asked impatiently.

"And what?"

"What was going on?"

"Life."

Aisling felt like screaming. "You know what I mean. What happened in Barrow in wherever?"

"Furness. As in Shadrach, Meshach and Abednego. Only spelt differently." He paused while Aisling fumed silently at her end of the phone. "No? What it is to belong to an unholy generation. Shadrach, Meshach and Abednego: the three young men who got thrown into the fiery furnace in the Book of Daniel? Ah well, knowledge may not always be power and you must have numerous other qualities, some of which will no doubt strike me if I think long enough."

"What happened in Barrow?" Aisling asked slowly through gritted teeth.

"Didn't I tell you? The *Apocalypse*, carrying spent nuclear waste from Italy, had already docked by the time I got there (despite Greenpeace, I fear), but there was no sign of Florence."

"Where is she, then?"

"I don't know." For once, John Smith sounded serious.

"She could be on her way home, or she may have decided to go back to Sellafield, but..."

"But what?"

"Someone I talked to said she'd seen Florence yesterday evening. She thought it very strange: she was walking up a side-street arm in arm with a couple of men."

Aisling felt as if a weight a lot heavier than Mulligan had been lifted off her shoulders. John Smith had obviously been stringing her along and she'd fallen for it, expecting him to say that Florence had been captured by Shavitov and Lerntowski. She grinned. "There must be something in the air: first Seamus falls for Antonia Browne, and then Florence goes off with two strange men. And you lot worry about *our* generation!"

John Smith sighed. "Why is it women see romance everywhere? Maybe I should have told you that this friend of hers just happened to mention that one of the men she was with was built like a gorilla and wearing a black suit and a bowler hat. Does that ring any bells?"

Aisling felt as if a load of rocks had crashed down on top of her again. "Shavitov! No. She must have made a mistake. I mean, even if he isn't dead—and you saw him die in Iceland too, didn't you?—it'd be an awful coincidence that he'd be in whatever you called it, Barrow-in-Furness, last night. The other man wasn't small and thin, was he? Like Lerntowski?"

"No. He was apparently a tall, blond fellow. But I don't know if I wouldn't prefer to think it was Lerntowski—at least he puts some sort of brake on our foul-minded fat friend."

"Florence *knows* Shavitov," Aisling objected. "She wouldn't go off with him."

"She might have had no choice, Aisling. Walking arm in arm might mean more than it seems."

"You mean she's a prisoner? What are we going to do? We have to rescue her!"

"I've already alerted the British police but, without more proof, there's not a lot they'll do, even for me. So I intend to follow up any leads myself."

"Peter and I will get the next boat over. We'll help you look for her."

"No. You stay where you are. I'm sending over a friend of mine from Greenpeace to talk to you. She'll tell you what we think is happening and you can take her up to meet Seamus. Her name's Deirdre, incidentally, though not of the sorrows. I'll ring myself as soon as I have more news; after all, Florence's friend might have been mistaken. Don't forget to give my love to Mulligan and remind him that gluttony (otherwise known as greed) is one of the seven deadly sins."

"But..."

John Smith hung up.

□

Later that evening, the phone rang again. Aisling rushed to answer it.

"Hello? To whom am I speaking?" It was a male voice with a plummy English accent.

"Aisling Daly. Can I help you?"

"No. I'm frightfully sorry but I appear to have the

49

wrong number."

The phone went dead.

"Who was that?" Peter had followed her out into the hall. "You look worried. Was it more bad news about Florence?"

"It was a wrong number. But it was very strange..."

"You don't think it was S.K.U.N.K., do you?"

Aisling looked at him in dismay. "No," she said firmly. "It was just a wrong number. As soon as I gave my name, he rang off."

The phone rang once more. Aisling and Peter stared at it.

"Do you think it's him?" Aisling whispered.

"Are either of you going to pick up that phone or are you going to leave it to ring all night?" Mr Daly shouted from the sitting room.

Aisling gingerly lifted the receiver. It was a woman, this time. "Hello? Is that Aisling? Good. This is Deirdre. Did John tell you I was coming over?"

Aisling breathed a sigh of relief. "Well, yes. We didn't think you'd be here so soon."

"I flew over—there's no time to be lost. I'm phoning from Dún Laoghaire. Can you and Peter meet me this evening?"

"Why don't you come here?" Aisling suggested. "We've got a spare room and I'm sure Mum won't mind." She suddenly remembered that Peter had the spare room. How many guests would her mother put up with? She waited, hoping that Deirdre would say she'd made other arrangements.

Deirdre hesitated. "John told me to be very careful.

He suggested I meet you in some public place, rather than go to your house. Maybe he's being too cautious, but if S.K.U.N.K. are watching you and Seamus, he thinks it better that they shouldn't know I've arrived."

"S.K.U.N.K.? Are they here?" Aisling looked anxiously at the glass panel in the front door, black now with the darkness outside. Were Shavitov or Lerntowski or any other of the S.K.U.N.K. agents hiding outside the door, listening to her on the phone? She felt shivers run down her spine at the thought.

"I don't know. But, just to be on the safe side, could you meet me at McDonald's in Dún Laoghaire? I'm wearing a green-and-blue anorak and I've an orange rucksack with me. I'll try and sit near the door. If you think you're being followed, just walk past and I'll get in touch with you again tomorrow. Okay?"

"Fine," said Aisling. "McDonald's in half an hour."

□

As they left the house ten minutes later, a taxi screamed into the street and stopped opposite Aisling's front door. A tall, thin young man leapt out. Aisling stared at him. His blond hair was cut short, his grey trousers had a knife-edge crease, his brown leather brogues sparkled in the light of the street lamp overhead. When his tweed sports jacket flapped open, a shocking pink waistcoat gleamed suddenly over a purple shirt and a broad purple-and-pink tie. He paid the driver and rushed over to them.

"Aisling Daly, I presume?" he asked. His accent was English—just like the mysterious caller on the telephone.

"No!" Aisling said quickly.

The man acted as if she hadn't spoken. "I'm absolutely delighted I caught you. I'm looking for Deirdre Callaghan. You wouldn't, by any chance, know where she is, would you?"

Peter opened his mouth. Aisling kicked him quickly. "No. We don't know any Deirdres. Sorry. Come on, Peter. We're going to be late." She dragged him down the road.

The man followed. "You absolutely must know Deirdre," he insisted. "Your number was the only Irish number in her little address book that I got to have a look at. I know she didn't have a name beside it, but you answered when I rang the number and very kindly gave me your surname; so I just had to look up a phone book to find your address. Pretty clever, eh?"

The phone conversation made sense now. Aisling wondered how she'd been so stupid as to tell him her name—but how could she have known it was someone from S.K.U.N.K. asking? They had to get rid of him somehow before they met Deirdre. "I'm sorry," she repeated. "I don't know who you think I am, but it must have been a mistake. I suggest you find a phone box and try out other numbers which might be like mine. Unfortunately, we're going late-night shopping and haven't time to help. Goodbye."

"You're going shopping? I'll come with you. I'm sure Irish shops are absolutely delightful."

Neither Peter nor Aisling answered, and they continued to cut him dead as they walked in silence along the seafront to Dún Laoghaire. He didn't seem to mind. He hummed a tune to himself quite happily as he strolled along beside them. Rats and double rats, Aisling thought. They'd have to shake him off before they met Deirdre, but how? She led them into the shopping centre. "There's the phone," she said, "if you want to try some other numbers. Bye."

"Thanks." He didn't move. Aisling looked round for inspiration. A crowd of people were just going into the lift. Grabbing Peter's arm, she dragged him in after her, just as the door was shutting.

"Now what?" Peter asked. "He can use the stairs."

"Let's hope the lift is quicker." She cursed silently as it stopped at every floor. Mothers seemed to take ages to manoeuvre their pushchairs out of it, old-age pensioners hobbled slowly to the doors, people came in at every stop. They pushed rudely past everyone to get out first at the third floor. Aisling looked towards the stairs: a pink waistcoat was just coming into view. "Quick. We'll just make it!" They raced round to the children's bookshop. Aisling's brother Kevin had a part-time job there and he was working that evening. She prayed that he'd be in the shop.

He was serving a customer.

"Kevin! I need to talk to you!" He glared at her and turned back to the customer. "That'll be four ninety-nine, please."

"We'll be in the back. It's urgent." She dragged Peter through a door at the back of the shop which led to a small store-room, and shut the door after them.

A young dark-haired woman was smoking a cigarette. "Hey! It's staff only in here. Out!"

"I'm Kevin's sister. I have to speak to him."

53

"Well, wait outside, then. Unless you want to lose him his job."

"Come on, Aisling," Peter said. He glanced back into the shop: the tall young Englishman was standing at the entrance, looking in. Peter shut the door again quickly. "He's there."

"We can't go out," Aisling pleaded with the young woman. "There's someone following us. I was hoping Kevin would let us out by the fire-escape." She looked at the fire-door behind them. "You wouldn't...?"

The woman stared at her thoughtfully. "What have you kids been up to? You haven't been stealing, have you?"

"No. I told you, I'm Kevin's sister Aisling. And we're just trying to get away from this man who was pestering us. Please..."

The woman hesitated. Then she stubbed out her cigarette. "Wait here—I'll get Kevin."

Two minutes later they had escaped through the fire-doors and were at the front of the shopping centre. There was no sign of the tall young man. Crossing the street, they ran up to McDonald's.

7

Deirdre

A girl of about seventeen, with curly brown hair and wearing a green-and-blue anorak, was sitting beside the door. She smiled hesitantly at them as they went in.

"Are you Deirdre?" Aisling asked.

"Aisling? Thank goodness. I thought you'd be here before now. I was worried that something had happened to you."

"Something did. A man tried to follow us, a tall blond man. I think it was the same person who helped Shavitov kidnap Florence in England. John Smith told us he was tall and blond too."

Deirdre looked quickly out at the street. "Are you sure you've shaken him off?" she asked anxiously.

"Yes." Aisling frowned. "He knew your name. Do you know who he is?"

"No. But I wouldn't be surprised if he belonged to S.K.U.N.K. John Smith said he thought they might try something in Ireland, even though he strongly suspects the stolen spent nuclear fuel rods are some place else."

"He strongly suspects the stolen spent nuclear fuel rods are some place else?" Peter repeated with a grin. "That's as bad as *Roland der Riese am Rathaus von*

Hamburg trägt eine Rüstung aus Erz."

"Or *she sells seashells on the seashore*," Aisling suggested.

"It's not funny, though," Deirdre said. "If S.K.U.N.K. has stolen them, then the world is in grave trouble."

"Stolen what?" Peter asked. "I don't understand."

"A few of the flasks containing spent nuclear fuel rods for the THORP plant have disappeared," Deirdre explained. "John thinks S.K.U.N.K. has them."

"What's a thorp plant? Is it some sort of biological weapon?" Peter asked.

Aisling imagined a Jack-and-the-beanstalk-type vegetable soaring up into the sky. She thought of Shavitov climbing it, pulling his huge body up leaf by leaf, and grinned. A look at Deirdre's face sobered her.

"Sorry. I forget other people don't know about it. There's a new reprocessing plant being built at Sellafield: the Thermal Oxide Reprocessing Plant, otherwise known as THORP. It'll eventually reprocess spent oxide fuel sent to it from all over Britain and also from foreign nuclear reactors, especially Japanese and Italian ones."

"Reprocessing means making the waste fuel safe, doesn't it?" Aisling asked.

"Not exactly. What happens is that the unused uranium and plutonium are separated out so that they can be used again."

"For bombs?"

"Well, yes, but not necessarily. Mainly for nuclear power stations. The trouble is that when you reprocess solid nuclear waste it turns into liquids and gases which are highly radioactive and which may take tens of thousands of years to become safe, no matter what people do with them. That's why people who care about the environment are trying to have the THORP plant shut down."

"Oh." Aisling tried to think of something being dangerous for tens of thousands of years. It was like trying to imagine outer space: impossible.

"You said S.K.U.N.K.'s stolen some of the...what did you call them?" Peter asked.

"Spent nuclear fuel rods. They're put into huge flasks for safety while they're being brought to Sellafield from other reactors. We think some of these flasks, which were in a shipment from Italy, have been stolen by S.K.U.N.K. We asked Sellafield but, naturally enough," Deirdre's voice turned bitter, "they're hushing it up and refuse to admit anything."

"How did S.K.U.N.K. manage to steal them?" Peter asked. "There must be massive security, surely?"

"We think they substituted dummy flasks which were unloaded, as normal, at Barrow-in-Furness and are now waiting in Sellafield to be reprocessed. Because they're just being stored there until THORP's ready for them, nobody looked at them closely until quite recently. And then one of our people discovered that some of them are fake."

"And S.K.U.N.K. switched them?"

"As far as we can tell, the flasks were okay when they left Italy, so the real ones disappeared somewhere between Italy and there. Possibly off the coast of Spain. John is certain it was S.K.U.N.K. who stole them."

Peter drew in his breath sharply. "How dangerous

are they?" he asked.

"Pretty dangerous. We don't know exactly how many they have, possibly only a few. But even three or four would be enough to cause a huge amount of damage."

Aisling thought of the two S.K.U.N.K. agents she knew best, Shavitov and Lerntowski. Both men were utterly evil. They wouldn't care how many people they killed, or how much radiation they released, if it got them what they wanted. If they had these nuclear waste things... "What could they do with them?" she asked. "Would they be like a nuclear bomb?"

"Not exactly. But, if an accident happens, or the outer cover is pierced, the fuel rods will reach an incredible heat and start a mega-fire as well as leaking massive amounts of radioactivity into the atmosphere. It's terrifying."

"And you and John Smith have a plan to stop S.K.U.N.K. and need our help." Aisling wasn't sure whether she was pleased or not: helping to outwit S.K.U.N.K. had been exciting in the past, but it had been very scary too. "What do we have to do?"

Deirdre smiled. "Nothing. John and various governments and their security forces are trying to trace the stolen flasks. The reason I'm here is because he's worried about your godfather. John thinks S.K.U.N.K. might want to get Seamus as well as Florence."

"Why?" Peter asked. "Nobody's done anything to S.K.U.N.K. this time. I mean, we only found out yesterday that they were still around. So why would they be after Seamus and Florence?"

"Out of revenge, John thinks." Deirdre looked serious.

"Seamus has been responsible for stopping them twice recently, and I gather he's been fighting them for years. John thinks they're using Florence as a decoy, to try to lure Seamus into danger. Someone has to warn him as soon as possible. Will you take me to see him now?"

Aisling frowned. "There's a problem."

"Will he have gone to bed? Maybe we should ring first and ask if he'll see us?"

"You'll never get through to him. You'll only get Miss Antonia Browne with an 'e.' And she won't let you anywhere near Seamus. Especially at this time of night. 'He needs his beauty sleep, chicken,'" she mimicked nastily.

"So she's still there? John Smith told me about her. He tried to ring Seamus when he found out about Florence, but she wouldn't put him through. That's why he sent me over. I still think we should try to see your godfather now, though. We've lost a lot of time and S.K.U.N.K. will have to make a move soon, if they intend to harm him too."

"OK," Aisling agreed. "But don't say we didn't warn you if we don't get anywhere."

Deirdre suggested they take a taxi up to Dalkey Hill. They walked round to the rank in Marine Road. As she waited for the others to get into the cab, Aisling had a sudden urge to look round. There, standing across the road staring at them, was the tall man with the fair hair and the pink waistcoat. She jumped into the taxi. "Dalkey Hill," she told the driver. "As fast as you can. We're in a hurry."

"Are you now?" he asked with a grin. But he drove off

smartly enough, Aisling thought gratefully, as she stared through the back window. The blond man had run across the road and was getting into a second taxi.

"There's a taxi following us," she said. "Can you lose him?"

"What do you think this is? 'Miami Vice?'" The driver looked in his mirror. "That's Connor back there. Why would he be wanting to follow us?"

"The man he's got, his fare, we're trying to avoid him," Aisling explained. "Please!"

"Okay. Whatever you say."

Deirdre and Peter had seen the second taxi pull out behind them. "Is it the same man as followed you before?" Deirdre asked.

"We can't lead him to Seamus. We have to shake him off first."

The taxi driver grinned as he went through the lights on red and the taxi behind squealed to a halt behind them. "That'll upset Connor. He doesn't like people rushing the lights, sure he doesn't."

They roared in and out of Dún Laoghaire's side-streets until they were sure Connor's taxi had got well and truly lost, and then they headed for Dalkey Hill. "Ask me again, some time," the driver suggested as he pocketed the large tip Deirdre gave him. "It was almost as good as being on the telly. I'm going to have a right laugh at Connor when we get back to the rank." He roared off, leaving the three of them outside Seamus's house.

"Now what?" Peter asked. "Do we ring the bell?"

"No. Wait a minute," Aisling suggested. "Give me time to get round to the back of the house. The window to the downstairs toilet's usually left open and I can climb in there if you keep Miss Browne Cow talking at the front."

It worked. As soon as she heard the front bell ring, Aisling climbed through the window and jumped down into the small toilet. She peered out into the hall: Miss Browne was talking to Peter and Deirdre at the front door. She'd have to wait until the Cow had gone back to the kitchen before sneaking up the stairs. She listened to the conversation at the front door. "I wish to see Mr O'Toole," Deirdre was saying firmly. "You have no right to stop me."

"Oh yes I have, Miss. As his nurse, I say that he's not well enough to have visitors. If you want to leave a message, I'll see that he gets it as long as it's not something that will upset him. He's an old man, you know, chicken. We have to look after him."

"This is something personal," Deirdre insisted. "Tell him I have a message from John Smith. I'm sure he'll see me then."

"I'm afraid not, dearie. If it were a message from the Angel Gabriel himself, I wouldn't disturb him. He needs his sleep, the poor darling."

"But..."

"Goodbye, now, pet. Come back another day when he might be stronger. But I suggest you ring first, just in case."

The phone shrilled in the kitchen.

"Excuse me, chicken, I have to go." Miss Browne shut the front door firmly. Aisling held her breath as footsteps shuffled back past the toilet into the kitchen. She opened the door carefully. Now was the time to sneak upstairs, while the Browne Cow was busy on the phone. And then she heard what Miss Browne was saying!

8

The Plot Thickens

"**H**ello," Miss Browne's voice boomed from the kitchen. "Andrei! You shouldn't be ringing me here, pet. Are you sure Petrovich doesn't know you're meeting me? If he finds out, there'll be trouble, chicken, you know that. Yes, of course. You know you can count on me, pet. Yes. Tomorrow. We've chartered a plane. We'll be landing in Lourdes about eleven tomorrow morning. I just can't wait to see you again, dearest. Now promise me that you won't go and do anything silly until I get there, promise me that, will you sweetheart? Good. You do love me one teensieweensie bit, don't you? I love you too, Teddybear. Till tomorrow, then. And God bless."

Aisling heard the click as the receiver was replaced. She crept out of the cloakroom, tiptoed along the hall and stealthily climbed the stairs to the attic. Her heart was pounding so loudly she felt it could be heard all over the house. Please let Miss Browne stay in the kitchen, she prayed. At least till she'd had time to tell Seamus about the phonecall. He'd have to believe now that his fat Browne Cow was up to something! With someone called Andrei (otherwise known, she grinned, as Teddybear). And someone else called Petrovich wasn't to know. Andrei and Petrovich: the names nudged the edge of her

memory. She knew she'd heard them before somewhere...
Just as she reached the top landing, it came to her. Of
course! Andrei Shavitov and Petrovich Lerntowski! She'd
been right about Antonia Browne all along!

She burst into Seamus's studio without bothering to
knock. Seamus was sitting up in bed, sketching. He put
down the stick of charcoal he was using and glared at
her. "Is the house on fire?" he asked coldly.

"I've come to warn you! Florence has been kidnapped
by Shavitov, and the Browne Cow..." she caught Seamus's
eye, "I mean Miss Browne is in on it! And S.K.U.N.K.
have stolen a whole pile of nuclear waste thingies and
intend to blow up the world!"

"Hmph. May I ask how you've suddenly become a
repository for all this knowledge?"

"Sorry?"

Seamus sighed. "Much as I hate agreeing with anything that walking encyclopedia with verbal diarrhoea
says, John Smith is right: your vocabulary leaves a lot to
be desired."

"Florence is in danger and the world is about to be
destroyed, and you go on about my vocabulary!"

He looked at her quietly for a minute. "How do you
know all this? And have you any proof? Or is it only a
vague suspicion of that over-enthusiastic spy-merchant
with the extended vocabulary? And don't say 'sorry?' again
(especially since you're not): I mean John Smith."

"Somebody told John Smith that she saw Florence
being taken away by someone who looked just like
Shavitov..."

"*Somebody*," parroted Seamus. "*Someone*. And 'looking

64

like' isn't being. Not everyone can be perfect and some unfortunate people must, by the law of averages, share our fat friend's physique. Florence told me herself she might stay a few extra days over there; she's no doubt off protesting somewhere with one of her new colleagues."

"No she's not. John Smith's sure she's been kidnapped. And S.K.U.N.K. has almost certainly stolen some radioactive stuff and they're threatening the world with it. Don't you care?"

"Personally, I'd prefer a bit of proof before getting my knickers in a twist. That is what you young things say nowadays, isn't it."

Aisling resisted an impulse to strangle him. "Andrei is Shavitov's first name, isn't it?" she asked. "Your Miss Browne," she made the woman's name sound like slime, "was talking to someone called Andrei on the telephone just now: she was arranging to meet him in Lourdes. And somebody called Petrovich wasn't to be told. That's Lerntowski, isn't it? Petrovich Lerntowski?"

"Hmm. Yes." Seamus sat up and looked interested at last. "You're sure about this, child?"

"Positive. She was talking on the kitchen phone. Which reminds me. Why does the phone ring downstairs now and not here?"

"I wouldn't think that's any of your business."

"Has that woman taken away your phone?" Aisling insisted.

"Antonia is only trying to save me from being pestered. By people like you, in fact. How do you expect a man to get any work done with the likes of you rushing in and out like a revolving door? And besides," Seamus changed from defence to attack, "what were you doing eavesdropping on other people's private conversations?"

"I was hiding in the downstairs loo and couldn't help hearing her. It's just as well, too, that I did."

"I shall refrain from asking why you were hiding in the...er...cloakroom," Seamus sniffed. "I don't think I want to know."

"Will you listen to me for a moment? I definitely heard the Br...Miss Browne arranging to meet Shavitov in Lourdes. He must be taking Florence there."

"You still haven't convinced me that Florence is in any danger. As for Antonia, I'm not blind, you know. I am aware that you dislike her. I'm surprised, however, that you should find it necessary to make up such a highly unlikely story about her."

"But I *heard* her! And she was definitely talking to someone called Andrei. She called him Teddybear and sweetheart!"

"That's enough, child!"

"It's true! Just you wait! I'll bet she goes off to Lourdes tomorrow."

Seamus grinned suddenly. "She might indeed," he said pleasantly.

"So you do believe me?"

"Did I say that? Perhaps you'd better go. I think I hear Antonia on the stairs."

Sure enough, a loud panting on the landing announced Miss Browne's arrival. She pushed the door open and stopped short when she saw Aisling. She glared, then sank into the armchair at the side of the bed. "How did you get here?" she asked, when she had got back her breath.

"Aisling and I were just talking about Lourdes," Seamus said pleasantly. "The home of St Bernadette and her healing springs. St Philomena's Society," he grinned at Aisling again, "have arranged to take me there on a pilgrimage."

"A pilgrimage?" Aisling heard herself squeaking. "But you don't believe—"

"In travel?" Seamus didn't let her finish the sentence. "This will be an exception. After all," he smiled once more, "I am getting old and it's time I thought of my soul for a change."

Aisling stared at him. For as long as she'd known Seamus, which was all of her life, he'd never shown any interest in religion. Nor, for that matter, had he ever admitted to getting old. And here he was now, going on about pilgrimages and souls. Antonia Browne must be feeding him some sort of drug, she decided. She jumped as Miss Browne spoke to her.

"I didn't hear you come in, Aisling chicken?" She'd got over her surprise and her voice was as treacly as usual again.

"Oh. Didn't you?" Aisling asked innocently.

Miss Browne smiled, but the look in her tiny brown eyes was deadly. "We mustn't tire our grandfather, must we? Especially as he has a big day tomorrow with all that travelling. I think it would be a good idea if you went home now, pet, and left him to have a little rest." Syrup oozed from her voice. "I'm sure, as you managed so well to see yourself in, you'll manage to see yourself out. And remember to say a prayer for your grandad.

Every little bit of prayer helps."

"Bye, Aisling. I'll bring you back some holy water," Seamus grinned at her.

Aisling glared at him, turned her back and stormed out on to the landing. If he wanted to be like that, why should she bother? If S.K.U.N.K. were trying to kidnap Seamus, they were welcome to him.

As soon as the door closed behind her, she regretted her rashness. It was all very well being mad at Seamus, but she couldn't really leave him to be kidnapped by Miss Browne. She had to try to warn him or convince him to take herself and Peter along.

She pushed the studio door open again and found herself staring straight into Miss Browne's large bosom. "Yes, chicken?" The honeyed voice boomed down at her. "Have we forgotten something, then?"

"I just realised how right you are," she said, with as much smarmy selfrighteousness as she could manage. "Prayer does help. Peter and I were just saying how much it means to us both and how we'd just love to go to Lourdes on a pilgrimage." *Irish schoolgirl wins Oscar for acting*. She hoped Miss Browne and Seamus were falling for it. "Please can we come with you? It would be a marvellously spiritual experience."

Seamus looked at her thoughtfully.

Aisling turned to Miss Browne. "Please," she said again. "I'm sure St Philomena's Society wouldn't mind us coming along. We could help with the aged and infirm. We're both very good with old people; after all, I've put up with...I mean I've helped to look after Seamus for years now."

There was a silence. Antonia Browne looked at Seamus. Seamus scratched his head with his piece of charcoal, leaving a black streak. Then he seemed to make up his mind. "And a fine job you made of it," he grunted. "With you as a helper, anyone even slightly under the weather would find death an easy option. If you want a bit of religion, I suggest you go to church for a change. Now, get out. I have things to do."

"What about Florence, then?" Aisling asked quickly. "What are you going to do about her?"

Seamus frowned.

"Is something the matter with Florence, pet?" Miss Browne asked sweetly.

"Aisling here thinks she may have got herself into some trouble."

"Oh dear. Oh, I *am* sad to hear that. But she's in England, isn't she? Surely you can't be expected to help her from here, chicken?"

"She's probably in Lourdes by now," Aisling said pointedly, looking straight into Miss Browne's piggy little eyes.

Miss Browne didn't blink. "Well, in that case, we can see her there tomorrow, can't we, pet? And now, we heard your grandfather asking you to leave, didn't we? It's not good for him to upset himself. I think you'd best go."

"But S.K.U.N.K. are waiting for you in Lourdes, Seamus!" Aisling tried one last appeal. "Don't let her talk you into going!"

Seamus stared at her. "I've had enough of this," he said coldly. "Out!"

Miss Browne stood up and opened the door. "Goodbye,

chicken, and God bless."

"And God bless you too, chicken," Aisling muttered as she thumped downstairs. Now what were they going to do?

Peter and Deirdre were waiting for her out of sight of the house. As they walked down the hill towards Dalkey, Aisling reported on the proposed trip to Lourdes and told them about the telephone conversation she'd overheard.

"So John was right," Deirdre said. "S.K.U.N.K. do have a plot to get even with Seamus and Florence. It wouldn't surprise me if Shavitov's taken Florence to Lourdes, if that's where he's meeting your Miss Browne."

"That's what I thought. Seamus just wouldn't believe me. That fat cow seems to have bewitched him."

"We'd better alert the French police," Deirdre suggested. "We'll have to ask them to put a tail on Antonia when she lands in Lourdes and hope that she leads them to Shavitov and Florence."

"Fine. How do you suggest we do that?" Aisling asked. "Ring up Interpol and say we think a group of pilgrims are part of an international plot to destroy the world and they've just by chance kidnapped an old man and his middle-aged sister? *Please, Inspector, won't you send a few men to Lourdes to spy on St Philomena's Society?* You have to be kidding."

"If you or I asked them, perhaps. But if John asks them, I think they might listen."

"Might!" said Aisling.

"How would we get in touch with John Smith?" Peter asked. "We don't know where he is. I think we should try to stop that woman taking Seamus to France. I know that won't help Florence, but at least it'll keep Seamus out of danger."

"How?" Aisling asked again. "I hate to be a wet blanket, but what do you suggest? You know Seamus: once he's made up his mind to do something, nothing will make him change it. Don't think I didn't try. The only way we could stop them would be for us to kidnap Seamus ourselves. But how on earth do we do that? I wish John Smith were here instead of gadding about in France or Spain or wherever; he'd be much more useful."

"John gave me a number where I can reach him," Deirdre said. "I'll get him to ask Interpol for help."

"Oh." For a moment, Aisling felt let down: why had John Smith trusted Deirdre and not her? She took a hold of herself. What did it matter, as long as they could get in touch with him? "Come back with us," she suggested. "You can phone from my house."

Deirdre hesitated. "I don't know. What about that fellow who was following us? He knows where you live. He could be waiting for you to come back."

"Rats," Aisling said. "What are we going to do, then? I mean, Mum'll go spare if we're not home soon. She'll be worrying already, it's so late."

"You go home," Deirdre suggested. "If he's there, then at least he'll be kept busy watching you and he'll leave me in peace to contact John. I'll find a bed and breakfast place in Dún Laoghaire somewhere and phone from there. I'll give you a ring in the morning and let you know what's happening. Okay?"

"*Prima*," said Peter. "Once John Smith's involved, I'm sure things will sort themselves out."

71

"Mmm," Aisling was more doubtful. "Perhaps."

She and Peter got off the bus in Sandycove and left Deirdre to continue on to Dún Laoghaire.

"Do you trust her?" Aisling asked.

"Who? Deirdre?"

"She could be anyone. S.K.U.N.K. even."

"She's a friend of John Smith's."

"We've only got her word for that."

"Do you mean you think she's *not* a friend of John Smith's?"

"I don't know!"

Peter shrugged. "Well, we can't get in touch with him and ask him so we'll just have to hope she is. More to the point, do you think she's right that that man will be watching your house?"

Aisling jumped. She'd forgotten about the tall blond stranger. She looked carefully along the road: it was deserted. "No. He's obviously given up. Thank goodness for that. I don't think I could cope with any more excitement this evening. I don't know about you, but I'm famished. I hope there's something decent in the fridge."

"You sound as bad as Mulligan." Peter grinned as he held the gate open for her.

Someone stepped from the shadow of the holly bush in Mrs Daly's front garden.

"You took your bally time," the tall fair Englishman said angrily. "Now, will you tell me what you and Deirdre have been up to?"

Aisling could have kicked herself for being so careless. She might have guessed S.K.U.N.K. wouldn't give up. She looked round for help, but the street was deserted:

even Mrs Clery across the way was having an evening off. They'd have to deal with him alone.

"Excuse me," she said firmly, and tried to push past him.

He grabbed her arm. "I'm not playing games, you know. I want to discover what's going on."

Aisling tried to pull herself away. The man held on tightly. Peter just stood and stared.

"Look, I'm actually on your side," the man said. "I'm with the Atomic Energy is Good Society, otherwise known as AEGS. Honest," he insisted as Aisling looked at him suspiciously. "I give you my word as an Englishman and a gentleman." With his free hand, he rooted in the inside pocket of his suit and brought out a plastic-covered identity card. "Here," he said, thrusting it in front of her face. "Read it."

Aisling read: Peregrine Montefiore. Atomic Energy is Good Society (UK Branch). 13A Finchley Park, London.

"So?" she asked rudely. He must think her a right idiot if he hoped she'd fall for that. And S.K.U.N.K. used all sorts of disguises.

"Why don't we go in and talk about it?" he asked.

Aisling saw her chance. "Okay," she said. "Come on, Peter." She tried to pull her arm away, but the man held tight. "Fine," she thought. "Have it like that." She led the three of them up the path to her front door and rang the bell.

Mrs Daly opened the door.

Aisling pulled her arm free and dashed inside. Peter followed her. Mrs Daly stared in surprise.

"Good evening," the man said, very politely. "Mrs Daly,

73

I presume? Peregrine Montefiore." He put out his hand.

Mrs Daly looked from him to Aisling. "What's going on?"

"Don't let him in, Mum," Aisling said quickly. "He was hiding in the bushes and jumped out on us as we came home. He must be one of these flashers or something. Shut the door and call the police."

Mrs Daly looked alarmed and tried to shut the door. The man put a foot in it. "Please, Mrs Daly. You're making a big mistake. I am an English stockbroker and I work with AEGS."

"Eggs?" Mrs Daly repeated. "*Eggs?*"

"The Atomic Energy is Good Society. Look, here's my card." He waved it wildly in front of her.

She frowned. "Please take your foot out of my door," she said coldly. "If you believe atomic energy is good, then I can't help you. Good day."

"But..."

"Aisling, go get your father."

The Englishman looked pained. "It's perfectly all right," he said. "I was just about to take my leave. Be a good girl and ask Deirdre where the spent fuel rods have got to," he shouted to Aisling as her mother shut the door. "I'm on the same side as yourself, actually..."

Anything else he might have said was cut off by the slam of the door.

9

Pilgrims

A isling was running down a long dark tunnel. Suddenly, a door opened in front of her and Antonia Browne oozed through it like a gigantic slug, with one of Florence's pink lace-edged pinnies tied round her bloated middle and Florence's crossbow in her hand. "You can't get away, chicken," she gloated, as Aisling tried to dribble a radioactive hockey ball past her. Aisling heard heavy footsteps behind her and, before she could turn, a pair of huge hairy hands closed round her throat. She choked, pulling at the hands, trying to free herself.

There was an angry miaow and something bashed her across the nose. She opened her eyes. Mulligan was lying on top of her with his head and front paws poking out of the duvet. He gave a quick lick to the paw he had struck her with and glared at her with baleful yellow eyes.

"It's okay, Mulligan. Calm down. I was only dreaming." She felt her face. There was no blood, so at least he'd had the sense to keep his claws in. She pushed him back down under the duvet where he growled complainingly, turned round a few times, kneading her stomach like an over-conscientious bread-maker, and crashed down on top of her. The duvet started to move gently up and down, the movement accompanied by a muffled purring.

She turned on her light and looked at the clock. It was six-thirty. She tried to get back to sleep, but all she could think of was Antonia Browne and Shavitov and their plan to kidnap Seamus. Was the Englishman Peregrine Montefiore part of it? Nobody could be born with a name like that: he just *had* to be a S.K.U.N.K. agent. He obviously knew Deirdre; did this mean that she was working for S.K.U.N.K. too? Aisling wished she could believe that Deirdre was genuine and had really warned John Smith. Maybe, if she had, the French police would be waiting for the plane at Lourdes and would arrest Miss Browne and Shavitov—and Lerntowski, too, if John Smith had found out what they planned and had followed them there. Maybe they'd rescued Florence already? She crossed all her fingers and hoped so.

Another thought struck her: what had Peregrine Montefiore done after they'd got rid of him the night before? Had he come back? Was he watching her house now?

She edged out from under Mulligan (who rolled off her with a complaining mutter, halfway between a squeak and a snarl, and then went back to sleep again) and crept to the window. She imagined the headlines in the *Irish Times* and grinned: *Terror at Dalkey house! Irish schoolgirl hockey-player besieged by mysterious Englishman!* Only it wasn't funny. She opened the curtains a crack and peered out. There was a car parked outside Mrs Clery's house with a man in it.

The man started the engine and the car moved off. So much for that.

She snuggled back into bed, putting an arm around Mulligan and hugging him tightly for comfort. Her thoughts continued to buzz around uselessly like trapped bluebottles. Maybe Peter was right and they should try to stop Seamus from going to Lourdes. But how? They couldn't tie him to his bed or lock him into the house or drug him or...Drug him! She sat up. They'd been doing poisonous plants in biology just the other day. What was it Mrs Healey had told them? Foxgloves were poisonous and so were laburnum seeds and rhubarb leaves. If she didn't use too much, just enough to make him ill...*Sandycove schoolgirl wins first prize at Young Scientist of the Year Exhibition with project on plant poisons.* Her mother was forcing some rhubarb under an old bucket in the garden. If she went out now and picked a few rhubarb leaves, before anyone was awake, she could boil them up and make a liquid (that was probably the best way to do it) and then take it up to Seamus's house and reheat it and put a couple of teabags in it and a lot of sugar and hope that he wouldn't notice the taste. She sighed. Who was she kidding? Even if she could make a drink out of rhubarb leaves, how was she going to get it into his tea, with Miss Browne fussing around like an over-anxious walrus; and, even if she did, how would she know how strong to make it? If it was too strong, he might die (and much as he infuriated her, killing him would hardly be the best way to save him from S.K.U.N.K.); if it was too weak, it wouldn't harm him at all.

And, even if by some miracle they managed to stop Seamus from going to Lourdes, there was still Florence to think of. How were they going to save her?

Rats, she thought. Rats to the power of four hundred.

She got up and went through to the spare room. Peter woke with a start when she shook him. *"Menschenskind! Was machst du denn hier? Wie spät ist es?"*

Aisling sat down on the edge of his bed. "I've been thinking," she said. "We have to go to Lourdes."

Peter sat up and rubbed his eyes. "What? Are you mad?"

"We can't just let the Cow get away with it. We'll have to try to join the trip."

"Have you any idea how much that'll cost? And what are your parents going to say?"

"Great-Aunt Agnes left me some money in her will. Five hundred pounds. They made me put it in the bank 'for a rainy day.'" Aisling looked through the window at the lights still shining across the bay on Howth. She grinned. "I'd say it's raining now, wouldn't you?"

Peter smiled. "Okay, so we use your money. But how do we get tickets? And what about your parents?"

"I'll tell them Seamus asked us to go with him. And that it's educational. They always fall for that. As for the tickets, we'll ring the airport and see. It's worth a try, anyway."

"What about passports and things? Have you got one?"

"Yes, thank goodness. We had to get one of these purple European things when we went off to play in the international schoolgirl hockey tournament in Brittany last autumn. I was in the Junior A team." She tried to sound modest about it.

"Did you win?"

"Er...not exactly. The point is, we both have passports and we have money, so all we need are tickets. Let's go down and ring the airport."

☐

"A flight to Lourdes this afternoon? One moment. Ah yes, there is one: a chartered flight organised by St Philomena's Society."

"Are there any free seats on it?" Aisling drummed her fingers tensely on the phone shelf. Mulligan, thinking this was an invitation, leapt up and wound himself round her neck.

"That's strange," the woman said. "There were quite a few empty seats on that flight, despite room being made for a stretcher, but there seems to have been a last-minute rush for them. Hold on a minute now...how many seats did you say?"

"Two." Aisling flinched as Mulligan licked her ear with a tongue like rough sandpaper.

"You're lucky. There's just two left. What are the names, please? Fine. Be at the airport an hour before take-off. Goodbye."

Aisling put the phone down and looked at Peter. "That's the tickets booked. Now to persuade Mum and Dad."

☐

"But it would be putting the money to good use! I mean, going to Lourdes would be a really worthwhile experience.

79

And it's not as if we'd be going alone: Seamus and the Br...Miss Browne would be there."

"I don't know," Mrs Daly said. "I realise you're disappointed at not being able to join Louise and her family on their boat, and you have given up a lot of your time to Seamus this Easter, but..."

"It would help my French. And it would be good for my religious development. And..." Aisling thought quickly, "I have to do a special project on Lourdes or Medjugorje or Fatima for Mr Sweeney for next term: it would be a great help actually to go there. And I could get all sorts of bits and pieces to paste into my project: you know, tickets and postcards and things. You're always telling me how interesting projects are and how I should try harder."

Mr Daly looked at his wife. They both sighed. "Well, I suppose, as it is educational and you're intending to go with a reputable pilgrimage and Seamus will be there to look after you, and as you're both on holiday..."

Neither Peter nor Aisling had thought it would be so easy.

Mrs Daly ran them to the airport.

"You don't need to come in," Aisling said. "We'll manage fine. It'll do us good to stand on our own two feet." This was one of Mrs Daly's favourite phrases and it worked.

They checked their rucksacks in and looked round. So far there was no sign of Antonia Browne or Seamus. "Why didn't you check that bag in too?" Peter asked, as Aisling humped a heavy holdall through to the departure lounge.

Aisling opened her mouth to say something and changed her mind. She smiled. "It's OK," she said. "It's not really that heavy." She seemed anxious, however, when she had to put it on a conveyor belt to pass through the scanner; it wobbled when she put it down and she seemed relieved to get it back safe and sound at the other end. She caught Peter's eye and grinned embarrassedly. "It's just something I prefer to have with me."

Other passengers for Lourdes were already waiting in the departure lounge. They were nearly all old or infirm, Aisling noticed: just the sort of people a genuine organisation, such as St Philomena's Society pretended to be, would take on a pilgrimage. She wondered if they were S.K.U.N.K. agents, or whether S.K.U.N.K. had just hired a lot of geriatric actors. They stared at Aisling and Peter curiously. Aisling smiled back at them.

"All right then, ladies and gentlemen. Have we got everybody?" The voice sounded vaguely familiar. Aisling turned round: it was Father Quinn's housekeeper!

She nudged Peter. "There! I told you she was with S.K.U.N.K."

"She doesn't have to be," he whispered back. "She's in St Philomena's Society, remember."

"Huh," Aisling snorted.

Their flight was called and there was still no sign of Antonia and Seamus. "Where are they?" Aisling asked worriedly. "They'll miss the plane."

The rest of the pilgrims stood up and Father Quinn's housekeeper ushered them out of the departure lounge. She turned to look at Aisling and Peter. Her face creased in a frown. "Should I know you, children? Are you coming with us?"

"Yes," said Aisling.

"No," said Peter.

"Make up your minds, dears. The plane's just about to leave."

"There's no point in going if Seamus isn't here," Peter pointed out in a whisper.

"There's still Florence," Aisling answered him. "And we've got this far. I think we should go anyway."

"Well?" asked the housekeeper.

Peter shrugged. Aisling picked up her holdall and the two of them followed the rest of the tour down some stairs and out on to the tarmac where their plane was waiting.

☐

It was a small plane, bigger than the one Aisling had been in the summer before (when S.K.U.N.K. had been creating earthquakes and volcanoes up in Iceland), but much smaller than the jets sitting on the runways around them. Aisling shivered as she remembered how Chris's plane had broken up and how she'd had to jump out and parachute into the sea. She hoped this one would arrive safely.

The two of them were given a seat at the back of the plane, which was just as well, as Aisling's holdall was beginning to move about alarmingly. "You've got Mulligan in there!" Peter exclaimed.

"Shh! I know it's illegal to bring him abroad, but I'm

not going to chance meeting Shavitov without him. You remember how allergic he is to cats."

Peter grinned. *"Stimmt,"* he said. "I do."

"If he can just keep quiet until we take off, we should be okay."

"If," said Peter. "I hope you've given him plenty of food."

The plane sat on the tarmac. The old people talked quietly to each other. Mulligan turned round once again in the holdall. And still they didn't take off.

"What's keeping us?" Aisling asked impatiently.

"I don't know. Maybe they're waiting for someone else to come. There's still..." Peter counted, "five empty seats."

He was right. A couple of minutes later, the door opened again and two people got in. They spoke briefly to the stewardess and then moved along the aisle towards the back of the plane. Aisling gripped Peter's arm tightly: the late arrivals were Deirdre and Peregrine Montefiore!

Deirdre saw her and came up to take the vacant seat beside them. Peregrine sat down next to Father Quinn's housekeeper.

"How did *he* get here?" Aisling demanded.

"I don't know. I met him at the airport. John Smith suggested I try to get on this flight and suddenly there he was, taking this flight too. He's harmless, really. I've known him for ages."

Aisling stared at her. "He's the man who followed us yesterday! You must know that."

"Oh. Are you sure? I never saw the guy properly yesterday, but it can't have been Perry. He's not the type to play detectives and race around the town chasing taxis.

83

He's extremely law-abiding and," she made a face, "dead boring."

"It was him."

Deirdre looked down the plane at Peregrine, a puzzled expression on her face. "If you say so, I suppose I have to believe you. But if you knew Perry, you'd see how incredible it is."

Aisling didn't reply. Her mind was racing. Could Deirdre really not have recognised Peregrine the previous night? If she hadn't told him about the trip to Lourdes, how had he known to turn up for just this flight this afternoon? Both he and Deirdre had found empty seats and yet the woman at the airport had said that she and Peter had got the last two seats left. Were Deirdre and Peregrine working together? Had he made it so obvious that he was spying on them so that they would suspect him and trust Deirdre? It was quite possible: S.K.U.N.K. was capable of anything.

Deirdre fastened her seatbelt. "That's a relief. I thought we were going to miss it." She looked round. "Where's Seamus?"

"He hasn't arrived," Peter said.

"Oh. Does that mean he isn't coming?"

Aisling looked at her coolly. "He's probably figured the whole idea was a S.K.U.N.K. plot. He was obviously only pretending to be taken in by..." she had been about to say "all you lot"; she changed it to "...Antonia Browne."

If Deirdre was disappointed, she didn't show it. "That's probably just as well."

Aisling turned her back and looked out of the window. She was surprised to see an ambulance on the tarmac beside the plane. As she watched, its rear door opened and two nasty-looking men dressed in crumpled white uniforms came out, carrying a stretcher. Antonia Browne, wearing a paisley headscarf and her dark-blue belted raincoat, followed them. Aisling craned her neck to see if Seamus was on the stretcher, but she only caught a glimpse of red blanket and then the stretcher disappeared underneath her window. A couple of minutes later, the rear door just behind her seat swung open. She glanced round and then immediately ducked back out of sight. There was a bump as the two attendants laid the stretcher on the floor of the plane, just behind the row of seats she, Peter and Deirdre were on.

"That's right," grumbled a well-known voice. "Drop me like a sack of potatoes. If you two gorillas are angels of mercy, it's no wonder some people prefer to die at home."

"Seamus!" Peter exclaimed.

"Shh!" Aisling laid a warning hand on his arm. "Don't let him know we're here yet. Let's wait till we've taken off."

The two ambulance men sat down in two of the remaining empty seats. Aisling sneaked a glance at them: they both looked like bouncers at a night club (or what she'd always assumed bouncers at a night club would look like. Unfortunately, despite hints to Kevin, not to mention John Smith, she'd not yet managed to visit a night club). One of them had fair hair, the other brown, and both looked like all-in wrestlers. Certainly, neither of them seemed the sort of person any normal hospital would employ in its ambulance service. If she'd wanted proof that S.K.U.N.K. was running this operation, Aisling thought, she had it now.

"Are we all right there, chicken?" Antonia Browne whispered loudly behind them.

"No," snorted Seamus. "We are not. But I doubt if there's much we can do about it."

"We'll soon be there, pet. Just be patient." The plane engines changed pitch as the pilot taxied along the runway for take-off. "I have to go and sit down now. But I'll be right back as soon as we're airborne."

"Hmph," said Seamus.

Aisling and Peter pretended to be looking out of the window as Miss Browne took the aisle seat opposite them. The plane came to a halt, its engines whined in a crescendo until every bolt in the plane seemed to shake, and then it started to move again. The runway sped past. Aisling glanced across at Antonia Browne: she had her eyes tightly shut and was running the beads of a silver rosary through nervous fingers. Then the engine note changed and they were airborne.

Aisling watched the ground fall away beneath them. Dublin disappeared and appeared again through a gap in the cloud and suddenly they were in the middle of the cloud itself, a suffocating whiteness that swirled past the round cabin window. A few seconds later the sun was shining again and they were looking down on mountains of white candy floss. As the plane climbed, the mountains turned into what looked like acres of freshly-fallen snow, deep, brilliant white and crunchy; the sort, Aisling thought, you want to jump into with wellington boots on. The notice in front of her advising her to fasten her seatbelt switched off. She undid the buckle eagerly and stood up.

"Excuse me." She squeezed past Peter and Deirdre into the aisle. Antonia Browne opened her eyes, looked up and saw her.

"What the hell are you doing here?"

Aisling pretended to be shocked. "Really, chicken," she said sweetly. "What would St Philomena's Society think of language like that?"

A flush spread over Antonia's pudgy face. "I'm sorry, pet. But you took me by surprise. I thought your grandfather had said you were not to come on this trip."

"I wouldn't count on that," Seamus muttered from the floor behind them. "If either of her grandfathers was speaking to her, he must have been using spiritualism: they've both been dead for years. As for her *god*father, he's given up expecting to be listened to."

"Sorry, Seamus." Aisling squatted down on the floor beside the stretcher. "I told you we wanted to come with you."

"True."

"And maybe you'll be glad we did, eventually."

"I very much doubt it. But as long as you young things enjoy yourselves, I suppose that's all that matters. Whether you spoil everyone else's holiday or not is obviously unimportant."

He was impossible, Aisling thought. Here they were, risking their lives to help him, and all he did was complain. She looked at the two stretcher-bearers and Antonia Browne. If Deirdre was with S.K.U.N.K. too, along with Peregrine, that made odds of five to three.

(She tried to forget that the three were herself, Peter and a crippled old man.) On the other hand, if Deirdre did somehow turn out to be what she said she was, then they would be even, four on each side. Though how much use herself, Peter, Seamus and a girl like Deirdre would be, compared to two all-in wrestlers, Peregrine and a fourteen-stone female battleaxe, was not something she wanted to work out.

Two children and famous Irish artist die mysteriously on charter flight to Lourdes! she thought wryly.

Surely S.K.U.N.K. wouldn't dare?

10

Flight to Lourdes

A isling's thoughts were interrupted by an angry
miaow. She went back to her seat: the holdall
was wriggling about like a jumping bean. She opened
the zip. Two orange ears, two angry yellow eyes, a
twitching pink nose and four rows of thick white bristles
emerged. The nose sniffed, and then the whole of Mulligan
erupted from the bag like furry orange milk boiling over
the rim of a pot. He gave her a filthy look, scrambled up
the seat, tottered for a moment on the top of it, recovering
his balance, and then crashed down on to Seamus's
stomach.

Seamus swore. "That is the final straw. I thought I
was getting away for a bit of peace and quiet and find
that the two of you have not only followed me here like
blobs of chewing gum stuck to a jacket, but you've brought
that great orange monster with you. Get him off me!"

Aisling felt in her anorak pocket for the chicken
sandwiches she'd made before they left Sandycove. She
tore one into small pieces and put it on the floor of the
plane.

Mulligan didn't need an invitation. Using Seamus's
stomach like a trampoline, he leapt off the stretcher and
scoffed the sandwich in two seconds flat.

89

"You are a bold, bold girl!" Miss Browne had finally struggled from her seat and joined them. "Bringing a cat on a plane! Whatever next?"

"It's all right," Aisling said sweetly. "He likes travelling."

"I am going to call the stewardess and have him locked up in the baggage hold." Miss Browne looked down towards the front of the plane and raised a pudgy finger.

"It's hardly worth the bother, Antonia." Aisling still couldn't get used to how polite Seamus could be when he wanted to. "He's here now, so we might as well put up with him."

Aisling picked Mulligan up quickly and stuffed him back into the holdall. She put another sandwich in with him to keep him happy and closed the zip.

"I know," she said quickly before either Seamus or Miss Browne could start lecturing her. "You shouldn't take animals abroad because of rabies and it's a very sensible precaution, but he's the only thing..." She had been going to say that he was the only thing that had any effect on Shavitov, but decided not to; there was no point in warning Miss Browne that they knew what she was up to. "I just don't like going anywhere without him," she finished lamely.

"Then you should have stayed at home," Seamus pointed out.

Aisling seethed. But she could hardly remind Seamus in front of Miss Browne that the only reason she and Peter were there was to rescue himself and Florence, and that it was costing her most of her savings to do so.

"Move out of the way, pet," Miss Browne ordered. "I

want to settle your grandfather—sorry, chicken, your godfather comfortably."

"I can do that," Aisling said. "Why don't you go back to your friends?"

"In a minute, chicken."

Aisling had to move back into her seat as Antonia piled pillows behind Seamus and fussed with his blankets. "We'll be there before we can get a chance to talk to him alone," she whispered to Peter.

"Did you get through to John Smith?" Peter asked Deirdre quietly.

"Yes. He said he'd deal with it," Deirdre answered equally quietly. "Whatever that means."

Aisling looked out of the window at the mass of white cloud beneath them. Now and again a gap appeared, revealing a patch of dull grey water: they must be over the sea, she thought. She wondered how much further they had to go. If John Smith was waiting for them at the end of the journey, then everything might still be all right, even with the two muscular ambulance men sitting across the aisle from them and Miss Browne keeping watch over Seamus like a broody hen. She glanced down the plane: Peregrine was still deep in conversation with Father Quinn's housekeeper and seemed unaware of their presence.

But then, after they'd all been given lunch on plastic trays, he stood up and came down the aisle towards them. "Deirdre," he said urgently. "It's dreadfully important that I talk to you before we land." He saw Peter and Aisling. "What on earth are you two doing here?"

"They're joining Aisling's godfather on the pilgrimage to Lourdes," Deirdre said calmly.

He glared at them. Then he turned back to Deirdre. "I absolutely must talk to you."

"Go ahead."

"No, seriously. Look," Peregrine's pale eyes flashed. "I do actually admire your idealism and all that, but you really have to face facts. We *need* nuclear energy. It's the only really sensible source of energy we have. And it's clean and non-polluting."

Aisling smiled sweetly up at him. "What about Chernobyl?" she asked.

"That was an accident. It won't happen again."

"Once was too often," Deirdre said quietly. "Do you realise that there are still places in Britain so contaminated from the Chernobyl fallout that sheep will be unable to graze there until well into next century? And have you any idea of the number of people in Russia who are still dying because of that 'accident'? And look at all the 'accidents' there have been in Sellafield itself over the years!"

"All right, so the nuclear industry's not perfect. But people get killed in coalmines and on oilrigs too. No fuel is completely safe."

Deirdre sighed. "There's no point in arguing, Perry. I'll never convince you and you'll never convince me, so we might as well go our separate ways."

"She means get lost," Aisling said helpfully.

"Thank you, Aisling. I know what I mean and I'd prefer to say it myself." Deirdre didn't sound pleased. She turned back to Peregrine. "When you've decided that

Greenpeace is right, look me up," she suggested.

"It's not just that, actually." Peregrine looked over his shoulder at the other passengers in the plane. "I have to talk to you about THORP," he whispered.

"What about THORP?" Aisling asked loudly.

"What are you playing at, woman?" Seamus roared from behind her.

"Sorry, pet." Aisling looked over the back of her seat to see Miss Browne mopping soup off Seamus's shirt with a paper napkin. "The bowl slipped."

She turned back to find Peregrine glaring at her. She smiled sweetly at him again. "You were going to tell us about…"

"I shall speak to you later, Deirdre," Peregrine said quickly, before she could finish the sentence. He stood up, gave Aisling another filthy look, and went back to his seat.

Aisling looked at Deirdre suspiciously. "You're very friendly with that awful weed."

"I told you I've known him for ages. And he's not that bad, really. He's just misguided. All he thinks about is money and 'progress.' I keep trying to convince him that if people invested as much money in wind or wave power, they'd produce all the electricity we need without polluting the earth or using up all our coal and turf. But it's like talking to a brick wall."

"I don't care how harmless you think he is," Aisling stated firmly, "I *know* he's a S.K.U.N.K. spy."

Deirdre shrugged, opened her briefcase and took out a pile of papers. "Excuse me. I've some work to do."

Aisling glanced round the plane. The two ambulance

men were playing poker and Peregrine was chatting away again to Father Quinn's housekeeper. Behind her, Antonia sat with Seamus, who seemed to have fallen asleep. It had turned into a very boring trip.

The intercom crackled. The pilot hoped that they were having a pleasant flight and told them that they were just crossing the foothills of the Pyrenees and they should expect to land in Lourdes in another ten minutes.

Ten minutes! Aisling thought in horror. Somewhere, under all that cloud, Shavitov was waiting for them! She'd somehow managed to push this knowledge to the back of her mind, but now she shuddered and clutched the bag with Mulligan tighter to her chest. Mulligan miaowed angrily. Aisling looked round quickly, but nobody appeared to have heard. "Shh, Mulligan," she whispered as she carefully stowed the holdall on the floor between her feet. "Just be good. I'm so glad you're here."

Then they had to fasten their seatbelts again, the plane passed once more through white, swirling cloud, small foreign-looking houses flashed by underneath, patchwork fields, trees, hills with forests along their flanks. And then the runway rushed up to meet them. They had arrived in France.

"Now what?" Peter whispered as the plane taxied to a halt.

"I don't know. Try to stick close to Seamus. And let's hope John Smith has laid on a welcoming committee."

The two massive ambulance men carried Seamus's stretcher from the plane by the rear door. Antonia walked beside it, fussing over Seamus's blanket and making sure he was all right. Aisling, Peter and Deirdre followed them.

And Peregrine Montefiore, Aisling noticed, tagged on behind.

Once inside the airport, they waited impatiently for their luggage to come off the carousel and then followed Seamus's stretcher through to the customs hall. Seamus was allowed to go first: Aisling and Peter rushed after him through the green channel, followed closely by Antonia Browne, Deirdre and Peregrine.

"Un moment, Madame. C'est votre valise?"

Aisling looked round. Antonia Browne, her face beet-root, was opening her case in front of a customs official. Behind her, Deirdre and Peregrine fretted impatiently. She couldn't believe their luck.

"Come on," she urged Peter. She rushed across the arrivals hall, not caring how many people she bumped into, and got outside just in time to see the stretcher disappearing into an ambulance and the door closing behind it.

The ambulance roared off, its siren blaring, as she reached it.

"Rats, double rats and quintuple rats!" she fumed. "Where the heck is John Smith?"

11

Hot Pursuit

P eter and Aisling watched the ambulance leave. "I thought the police were supposed to be waiting for us," Peter said. "I don't see any, do you?"

"That proves it then," Aisling muttered. "Deirdre *is* working for S.K.U.N.K. And they've got Seamus. What do we do now?"

There was a sound of heavy breathing behind them. A hand fell on Aisling's shoulder. "Where is your godfather, pet?" Miss Browne's loud voice boomed.

Aisling whirled round. "You know where he is," she said accusingly. "He's been kidnapped by S.K.U.N.K."

"Kidnapped? What do you mean, chicken? And what has a skunk to do with it?"

Aisling looked at her in disgust. "Don't try that on. We know about you and Shavitov."

A blush started on Miss Browne's neck, spread across her four chins and turned her chubby cheeks bright pink. "Have you seen Teddybear? Where is he?" she asked eagerly.

"He's in that ambulance that's just driven off," Peter informed her.

"Quick!" Miss Browne pushed past a group of elderly ladies, members of St Philomena's tour, who were climbing into a minibus standing at the kerb. Aisling looked at Peter and pulled him after her into the minibus too. Deirdre and Peregrine, who had just come out of the airport, saw them and jumped in as well.

"Suivez cet ambulance!" Miss Browne ordered the bus driver.

He looked at her enquiringly.

"Je vous ai dit de suivre cet ambulance!" Miss Browne repeated in an atrocious French accent. Aisling thought of all the time Miss Colombe spent trying to get them to speak French properly. Maybe it was worth it after all.

The bus driver shrugged, put the bus into gear and moved off, leaving most of the members of St Philomena's pilgrimage standing on the pavement looking dazed. Aisling felt a bit guilty: if they had nothing to do with S.K.U.N.K. (and the more she thought about it, the less she believed that they could *all* be S.K.U.N.K. agents), it was a bit hard on them to have their tour-bus hijacked and be left stranded at a foreign airport. As she looked back, she saw Father Quinn's housekeeper join them. She found herself hoping they would be all right: if anyone looked like chickens, it was the group of elderly pilgrims gazing forlornly after them.

The ambulance was disappearing fast into the distance but the bus driver, egged on by Miss Browne (who ought to have been a warder in a prison, Aisling thought, the way she loved bossing people around), managed to keep it in sight. Soon they were racing along the floor of a flat valley.

"What's happening?" a lady with a blue rinse in her permed hair asked. "Why are we going so fast? And why did we leave the others behind?"

Miss Browne stood up. "We have just left the airport of Tol," she announced, in a fruity tour-guide voice. "We will be in Lourdes in just a few minutes. Notice the beauty of the mountains. They are called the Pyrenees and form the border between France and Spain."

"But what about Mary?" another lady asked. "What's happened to Mary?"

"And my husband John?" a third voice piped up. "I wanted to stay with John."

"The others are coming on a second bus," Miss Browne said quickly. "They will meet us in Lourdes. Now, I want you to look at the scenery. As you will notice, the people here don't fence around their fields but grow their crops in strips, as we used to do in the Middle Ages."

As her voice droned on, her charges quietened down and looked dutifully out of the windows. Aisling watched the ambulance ahead. Was Seamus safe? If Shavitov was with him in the ambulance, was he still alive?

Peter turned to Deirdre. She and Peregrine had taken the seats directly behind them. "I thought you said you'd told John Smith when we were arriving," he said. "Why was there nobody at the airport?"

Deirdre looked worried. "I don't know. I didn't even see what happened. They got Seamus, did they?"

Aisling gave Peter a dig in the ribs. "Don't talk to her," she mouthed. "She's with S.K.U.N.K."

"How do you know?" Peter whispered.

"It's obvious."

Peter was silent for a moment. Then, "What are we going to do?" he asked.

"I don't know," Aisling said angrily. She unzipped the holdall and let Mulligan out. He shook himself, dived down on to the floor and disappeared under the seat. There was a scratching sound and an unmistakable smell filled the minibus. Mulligan reappeared in the aisle between the seats, jumped back up on to Aisling's lap, put his front paws up on the edge of the window, pressed his nose to the glass and looked out. He, at least, seemed interested in the scenery Miss Browne was describing, Aisling thought. She tried to ignore him and look as though she couldn't smell anything strange.

"Really, Mulligan!" Peter said disapprovingly. *"Du bist ja schrecklich!* I'm ashamed of you."

Miss Browne's smile wavered, but she glued it firmly back into place. *"Voici Lourdes!"* she announced in her dreadful French accent. "Since the mid-nineteenth century, this little mountain town has been the sanctuary of the Marian visions. As you all know, Bernadette Soubirous, a little shepherdess, saw a vision of Our Lady in this very place in 1858. She was only fourteen years old. In 1933 she was canonised by Pope Pius XI and is now Saint Bernadette. We shall, during our stay, visit the mill where she was born, her father's house, the fortified castle of Lourdes and, of course, pray at the grotto itself..."

She continued her commentary as they passed through narrow streets of white-washed houses whose steeply-pitched slate roofs and wooden shutters reminded Aisling of the time she'd travelled through France to Switzerland with Seamus and Florence. That time they'd outwitted S.K.U.N.K. and got home safely. She wondered whether they'd be so lucky now.

The ambulance ahead slowed down and turned into a side-street. It drew up in front of a large house with an imposing front door.

"*Arrêtez-vous!*" commanded Miss Browne.

The bus driver stopped at the corner of the street. Everybody craned their necks to see what was happening. "Is that Saint Bernadette's house?" the lady with the blue rinse asked eagerly.

"What, pet?" Miss Browne jumped. "Oh. No. It's...It's..."

As she hesitated, the back door of the ambulance opened and the two stretcher-bearers got out. The end of the stretcher was visible at the back of the ambulance, but Aisling couldn't see whether Seamus was still lying on it. He could have been killed already, she thought, hugging Mulligan so tightly that he miaowed in protest. What on earth were they going to do? She imagined the headlines in the *Irish Times*: *Irish artist disappears in town of Saint Bernadette!*

One of the stretcher-bearers went round to the front of the ambulance to talk to the driver; the other knocked at the solid wooden door of the house.

Before Aisling realised what was happening, the ambulance suddenly zoomed away, knocking the first man over and leaving the other one standing at the door with his mouth wide open.

"*Est-ce que vous voulez que je suive l'ambulance?*" the bus driver asked in a bored voice.

Miss Browne hesitated.

"*Oui,*" Aisling and Peter said together.

The driver winked at them, put the bus into gear and roared down the narrow street. The second stretcher-bearer was just helping the first to his feet as they passed. Aisling grinned as they both rushed out of the way. The tall blond one looked up and saw her: the narrow eyes in his twisted face glared at her viciously. She stopped smiling.

The ambulance turned left into the next main street and drew up in front of a church. The bus driver, without waiting to be told, pulled in behind it.

Aisling stared at the ambulance. Seamus was in it! They had to do something.

She took a tight hold of Mulligan and turned to Peter. "You try and get into the back and see if Seamus is all right. I'll distract the driver."

"What if it's Shavitov?" Peter whispered back. "You can't take him on. He's dangerous!"

"Let's just hope he's still allergic to cats." Aisling tried to sound more confident than she felt. The thought of meeting Shavitov again made her stomach churn like a cement-mixer, but at least they had to *try* to help Seamus; they couldn't just leave him there to be carted off again whenever the ambulance decided to move on.

"Wait a minute," Miss Browne said as they stood up to get off the bus. "Where are you two children going?"

"We're getting off here," Aisling said politely. "Thank you for the tour."

Deirdre stood up too. "Wait for me," she said.

"And me," said Peregrine, standing up as well. "This might well be frightfully interesting."

Aisling looked at Peter in despair. How could they

101

save Seamus if half of S.K.U.N.K. came too? "Shouldn't you be getting your tour back to their hotel?" she asked Antonia Browne hopefully.

"Seamus is in that ambulance, isn't he?" Deirdre asked. "I think we should see if we can get him out."

"But..."

There was nothing Aisling could do.

They piled out on to the pavement, the elderly ladies following, no doubt assuming that this was part of their tour.

Peregrine marched firmly up to the back door of the ambulance and flung it open. The others rushed forward and peered inside.

Seamus was sitting up on one of the beds, glaring out at them.

"What do you think this is?" he roared. "The Moscow State Circus? If you have quite finished peering in at me like a bunch of morons at a caged chimpanzee, shut the door quietly as you go. I have things to do."

Aisling pushed her way to the front of the crowd. "Are you OK, Seamus?" she asked anxiously.

"Of course I'm OK, as you put it in that lamentable English of yours. Why shouldn't I be? And I might have guessed you would be the reason for all this interference. You and that blasted cat never did know when to keep your noses out of things."

Mulligan, as if he realised that Seamus was talking about him, leapt out of Aisling's arms straight into the ambulance. He jumped on to Seamus's chest and started to knead his claws into Seamus's Aran sweater.

"Get that blasted feline off me! And get out of here, all

of you! Go off and pay a visit to Saint Bernadette or something, but leave me alone!"

"It's all right, Grandad." A soothing voice came from the front of the ambulance. Aisling couldn't believe her ears. She looked past Seamus and there, to her amazement, was none other than John Smith.

"So you were here after all!" she said.

"Naturally," John Smith replied. "Didn't Deirdre tell you I was taking care of things?"

Aisling looked away in embarrassment. Peter, who had pushed through the crowd to join her, gave her a dig in the ribs. "There," he said. "I told you Deirdre was genuine."

"Are you all going to go away or shall I charge a viewing fee?" Seamus interrupted. He appealed to John Smith: "Can't you get rid of them?"

"Ah yes." John Smith smiled. He got down from the cab and came round to the back of the ambulance. Everyone turned to face him.

"Now, ladies," he said, smiling charmingly at the assorted old dears. "I have no doubt you wish to rendez-vous (an interesting French word that, meaning 'to render yourself' or hie yourself to a place, if you prefer) with your companions in prayer. Miss Browne here will escort you back to your hotel."

"But..."

John Smith cut her short. "St Philomena's Society would hardly countenance (an interesting word that, too: it means 'face', in its original, but has come to mean 'agree to'; quite fascinating, you must admit) your abandoning them here in the middle of nowhere. Quite.

Au revoir then, all of you. I look forward to renewing your acquaintance at a more propitious (from the Latin, meaning 'favourable,' Aisling) time."

He ushered the little old ladies back into the bus and gently but firmly pushed Miss Browne in after them, like stuffing a cork in a bottle, Aisling thought. "What hotel are you going to?" he asked.

"The Hôtel du Vieux Coq," answered the lady with the blue rinse.

"Alors, monsieur," John Smith pressed something into the bus driver's hand. "L'Hôtel du Vieux Coq."

"Bien, monsieur." The driver tipped his hat. *"Merci bien."*

"But..." Miss Browne squeaked again. The driver ignored her and the bus roared off.

John Smith watched it go. "A formidable lady, our Antonia," he said with a sigh. "One can't help admiring her."

"I can," Aisling muttered.

"I thought you were going to get rid of all these people," Seamus complained from inside the ambulance. "It still sounds as if you have half a football crowd there."

"Not at all, Grandad. Only four stalwarts, all set to storm the magic castle and rescue the fair maiden in distress."

"To do what?" Aisling asked.

"Oh ye of short memory. Have you forgotten Florence?" John Smith asked.

"Of course I haven't. You mean we're going to rescue her now?"

"Got it in one, Aisling. I keep saying your godfather

doesn't give the Irish education system the credit it deserves."

"But...Can I speak to you privately?"

"As long as it doesn't take all day." John Smith led her aside from the others.

"What about Peregrine?" Aisling hissed, as soon as they were out of earshot.

"What about who?"

Aisling indicated the tall Englishman who was leaning nonchalantly up against the side of the ambulance, his pink waistcoat glowing in the spring sunshine. "Peregrine Montefiore."

"You're pulling my leg, aren't you? Nobody has a name like that."

"He's one of *them*," Aisling said.

"Oh. One of *them*," John Smith mocked.

"You know what I mean. One of S.K.U.N.K."

John Smith looked at Peregrine thoughtfully. "Are you sure?" he asked. "I mean, you've been wrong before."

"He was spying on us at home. And he followed us to Lourdes. And, as you just said, nobody could be called Peregrine Montefiore. It has to be false."

"I've heard of sexism," John Smith said with a grin. "And racism. But that's the first time I've heard of nomenclaturism—from the Latin for name, I hasten to add."

"Will you be serious?" Aisling asked, practically screaming with frustration. "We have to find a way to get rid of him."

"I'll put Deirdre on to it," John Smith suggested. "Now, was that all you wanted to talk to me about? If so, let's get back to plan A: how to rescue Florence. At this rate we'll all be drawing our old-age pensions before we start."

They returned to the ambulance. Peregrine immediately rushed up to John Smith. "You seem to be in charge here," he said. "Have you any idea whereabouts in Spain these bounders have actually taken our nuclear waste flasks?"

John Smith winked at Aisling, who was making warning faces behind Peregrine's back. "No," he said. "Not exactly. I was hoping our fat friend might throw some light on the matter."

"I beg your pardon. Fat friend? To whom are you referring?"

"You don't know Shavitov? Ah. Then you have a treat in store. Now, to get down to business: Florence, I suggest, is probably in that house we stopped at back there. What are we going to do about it?"

"Get her out," Seamus said shortly.

"True, oh wise old man. But how?"

"I thought you were going to ask the police to help you?" Deirdre said.

"Indeed and I was. Only, when I asked, they said 'not today thank you' and suggested I was suffering from an advanced case of paranoia brought on by reading too many thrillers. The cynicism of today's public servants never ceases to depress me."

"It's frightfully important that we find these flasks," Peregrine insisted. "If it leaks out that they're missing, there's going to be an absolutely dreadful scandal."

"If what's in them leaks out," Deirdre said coldly, "there will be more than a scandal. There'll be a disaster."

John Smith held up a hand. "Quiet, children. Keep your lovers' tiffs till later. At the moment, as I said before, our first priority is to rescue fair Florence and we're obviously going to have to do it without divine intervention or the help of the local *gendarmerie*. Now, listen carefully, and I'll begin. This is what I have in mind..."

12

Trojan Horse

"**F**irst," John Smith said, "we have to reconnoitre (otherwise known as 'suss out,' I believe, in the films you young things rot your brains watching on television) the house back there. If they've been careless, there might be a window open through which Aisling, for example, might test her burglarious skills. I suggest you all wait here while I go and see."

He returned five minutes later. "S.K.U.N.K. must be under new management: that place looks as impenetrable as Fort Knox." He turned to Aisling. "Which…"

"Which is where the Americans keep their gold bars," she said quickly, before he could give her another lecture. "I know, I saw a film about it."

"Blessed be the cinema, for it shall spread enlightenment amongst the masses," John Smith intoned.

"So what are we going to do? " Peter asked. "We can't just abandon Florence to Shavitov."

"Did you ever hear the story of the Trojan Horse?"

Aisling groaned. "Are you sure you were never a teacher?" she asked. "Did it ever dawn on you that people don't want to be snowed under with useless information all the time?"

"No," said John Smith happily. "Fortunately not. To

continue. If you remember, Helen, a beautiful Greek princess (the face that launched a thousand ships and all that) was kidnapped by Paris, who, in this case, was not the capital of France but the son of the King of Troy. Just as our own dear Florence (who might be said to have prepared more than a thousand lunches, all of them excellent) has been kidnapped by Shavitov, who is no prince. But we can't have everything."

"Will you get to the point, man?" Seamus grumbled. "We haven't got all day."

"Sorry. Well, the Greeks laid siege to the town of Troy but couldn't get in, so they built a model of a huge wooden horse, filled it with soldiers and left it outside Troy's front door, so to speak. Naturally, the Trojans became curious and brought it inside; upon which, out sprang the Greeks all waving spears and bingo! They won."

"You're not suggesting we build a wooden horse, are you?" Aisling asked, not bothering to hide the scorn in her voice.

"No, oh best beloved. I am suggesting we use our ambulance for the same purpose." He took off his ambulance driver's jacket and cap and handed them to Deirdre. "This young gentleman here—Peregrine, did you say your name was?—Peter and myself will position ourselves outside the front door of the house back there. Give us a few minutes to get ready, then drive the ambulance round. You could do a bit of bee-baaing, just to get their attention. They will all no doubt come rushing out, thinking I've decided to bring Seamus back to them, having exhausted the delights of the town. We shall then knock them on the head and Mafeking shall be relieved

109

(though that's the Boer War, not the Trojan War, Aisling; I'd hate you to get your history muddled up)."

"Rats," Aisling said under her breath. "What do *I* do?" she asked out loud.

"You'd better stay in the ambulance with Deirdre. If the plan doesn't work, then drive off smartly before they get a chance to catch you too. Wait for the rest of us— say at the train station. If we don't turn up in the next hour or so, get back home as best you can."

"And what about my waste fuel flasks?" Peregrine asked plaintively.

"We'll worry about them when we've got Florence back. Okay?"

"I think Peregrine should come with us," Aisling said.

"Nonsense. It's nice to know you think Peter and I are supermen, but I don't fancy even the two of us taking on both these gorillas and Shavitov on our own. Are you any good at unarmed combat, Peregrine my son?"

"Yes, actually. I was an officer in the Cadet Corps when I was up at Oxford."

Aisling tried to draw John Smith aside. "He's with S.K.U.N.K.!" she whispered. "Don't trust him!"

"I won't." He jumped down from the ambulance. "Come on you two. Let's go! Give us three minutes, then make your entrance."

Deirdre and Aisling watched them disappear round the corner. The three minutes which followed seemed like the longest three minutes in Aisling's life. Deirdre drummed her fingers on the steering wheel while Seamus sketched away like mad in the back of the ambulance. She herself hugged Mulligan tightly. What if there were more than just the two stretcher-bearers and Shavitov in the house? What if John Smith and Peter were captured too? For all John Smith's confidence, it sounded the worst plan she'd ever heard of. She didn't see how it could succeed.

"That's it, girl. Three minutes. Off you go."

"Thanks, Seamus." Deirdre smiled weakly and started the ambulance. She switched on the alarm, did a U-turn and drove back to the street they'd been in before. Aisling saw John Smith, Peter and Peregrine standing against the wall of the big house, waiting. They looked terribly obvious, she thought worriedly.

Deirdre stopped the ambulance, but left the alarm on. She also left the engine running, Aisling noticed.

The front door of the house opened. The tall blond stretcher-bearer looked out. He called something over his shoulder and the other one appeared. They both came out of the house towards the ambulance.

Without giving herself time to have second thoughts, Aisling quietly opened the passenger door and, still holding Mulligan tightly, dropped down on to the road. The ambulance was between her and the house so, for the moment at least, she was invisible. She hoped.

She heard someone try to open the back door of the ambulance. Then there was a grunt and a thud. Still holding Mulligan, Aisling raced round the front of the ambulance, past an astonished Peter and in through the door of the house.

Peter followed her in. *"Um Göttes Willen!* What are you trying to do?" he hissed.

She looked back at the street: one of the stretcher-bearers was slumped in a heap on the road, the other was struggling with John Smith and Peregrine. "Come on," she said, keeping her voice low. "Let's find Florence."

"She could be anywhere," Peter whispered back. "Where do we start?"

Aisling looked round. They were in a dingy entrance hall. Stairs rose to a landing above and, in front of them, a passageway led to the back of the house. Halfway along this was an open door. As she tried to decide where to start looking, she heard heavy footsteps coming up the stairs towards the door in the passageway. She remembered that French houses usually had cellars: that door must lead to the cellar and someone was coming up right now!

"Quick!" she hissed. "In here!"

They darted into the room to the right of the hall. Aisling closed the door behind them until only a crack was left. She peered through it. The heavy footsteps got nearer. Aisling felt her heart begin to beat so loudly she was sure even the men fighting in the street would be able to hear it.

Even though she expected it to be Shavitov, she still got a shock when his huge form appeared in the hall, not two feet away from her. Her legs seemed to turn into soggy playdough. She cuddled Mulligan tightly. Thank goodness she'd thought to bring him with her.

And then she saw Shavitov draw a gun from his pocket and aim it at someone outside. She was tempted to close the door and pretend she hadn't seen him, pretend that she'd imagined the gun; after all, what good would it do if she and Peter were found as well?

But she couldn't just let him shoot John Smith.

With an enormous effort of will, she wrenched the door open and threw Mulligan at the huge fat man. Mulligan was already angry at being carted around like a parcel and held so tightly he could hardly breathe. Being treated like a rugby ball was the last straw. He landed on Shavitov with all his claws out, growling and spitting like a furry orange Catherine wheel.

Shavitov was taken by surprise. He fell over backwards. His gun went off, the bullets knocking pieces of plaster off the ceiling which swirled gently down to settle on top of him like dirty snowflakes. Mulligan raked a claw-filled paw across his face and jumped off him to squat, growling angrily, in the corner opposite Aisling by the front door.

Shavitov started to sneeze uncontrollably. His gun fell out of his podgy hand. Peter snatched it up. "I'll keep him here—you go and find Florence," he ordered her.

Aisling didn't argue. She raced down the stairs to the cellar. Shavitov had been down there, so that must be where they were keeping Florence.

"Are you there, Florence?" she shouted. "It's me! Aisling!"

"In here!" The voice came from behind one of two doors on the right. It was fastened by a long metal bolt. Aisling drew back the bolt and the door swung open to reveal a grimy washroom with two huge stone sinks, a big copper boiler, an old-fashioned washing machine and a mattress on the stone floor.

Florence was sitting on the mattress, calmly knitting a purple, navy and pink jumper. She looked up. "Why,

Aisling! How good of you to let me out. Are you sure you shouldn't be at school?"

She rolled up her knitting, placed it carefully in the tapestry knitting bag she took everywhere with her and stood up.

Aisling was horrified to see how frail and old she looked. "Are you all right?" she asked anxiously.

"Of course." Florence steadied herself against one of the stone sinks.

Aisling just reached her before she collapsed. She put an arm round her. "Do you think you'll be able to make the stairs?" she asked.

Florence smiled bravely. "How very silly." She took a deep breath. "I'm sure I shall. As long as we don't go too fast."

They had almost reached the top of the stairs when there was a loud *prriau* and Mulligan hurtled down towards them, nearly knocking Florence off balance again. She bent to pet him. "Mulligan! Are you here too? How lovely!"

"Come on. We have to get you out of here." Aisling pulled her up the remaining few stairs.

She froze as they came out into the passageway.

Peter was backed into a corner, the gun in his hand still pointed shakily at Shavitov. Shavitov had stood up and was inching towards him. "Give me zat gun, leetle boy. ACHOO! You knows you vill not shoot eet. ACHOO! Eef you are good leetle boy and gives it to Shavitov, Shavitov might only hurt you a leetle, yes? Eef not…" He broke off in a paroxysm of sneezing but this didn't stop him from edging ever nearer to Peter.

Peter stared at him, like a rabbit staring at a stoat. "Don't come any closer or I'll shoot!" he stuttered. "I swear I will!"

"Me, Shavitov, I does not believes you." Shavitov continued to inch forward.

Aisling looked round desperately for Mulligan. He caught her eye and dodged out of reach: he'd been used as a weapon once today already and had no intention of being chucked at anyone again.

"Shoot his leg, Peter!" she screamed.

Shavitov whirled round. "Ach so, eet ees you, leetle girl. Zees time I vill make you suffer for ze suffering you have done to me, yes? Zees time!"

"This time you will put your hands up and go and stand over by the wall there."

John Smith had appeared behind him in the doorway, seen what was happening, and grabbed the gun from Peter. Aisling had never been so glad to see anyone in her life. She would never complain about his boring conversation again, she decided, as long as he saved them from Shavitov now.

Shavitov's face took on an expression of such hate that Aisling stepped back behind Florence. John Smith raised the gun. Shavitov hesitated, sneezed again, then shrugged and put his hands on his head.

"All right now. Florence, you Peter and Aisling—and your feline secret weapon there—get back in the ambulance and wait for me. I'll just lock our fat friend up so he won't do any more harm."

"There's a room in the cellar," Aisling volunteered. "That's where he had Florence."

"Perfect. What's called poetic justice, Shavitov my old friend. Though why poets should be accused of wanting to get their own back like that, I've never known. Come on then, Fatso. Stand aside and let the ladies pass."

Aisling picked up Mulligan. Shavitov glared at her. "You just waits," he threatened. "I, Shavitov, vill make you suffer for zees, you leetle..."

"Tut, tut. No bad language now," John Smith warned him. "Down the stairs with you."

Aisling waved Mulligan in his direction as she passed him. She grinned as it set off another bout of sneezing.

While John Smith shepherded Shavitov down into the cellar, she helped Florence out into the street. The ambulance was still there, but there was no sign of either Peregrine or the stretcher-bearers.

She settled Florence in the bed opposite Seamus's in the back of the ambulance.

"And about time, too, woman!" Seamus greeted her grumpily. "I hope you realise that you've mucked up my holiday? If you'd stayed at home like any normal woman and looked after me, instead of gadding about protesting about nuclear power stations, I would be enjoying a tour of Lourdes instead of sitting about here, waiting for someone to come and tell me what's going on."

"It's nice to see you again too, Seamus," Florence replied. "I'm sorry you've been put out, but there are some things, and nuclear power stations are one, that it's worth a little inconvenience to protest about."

"A little inconvenience?" Seamus exploded. "You call this a *little* inconvenience? I've had to put up with Aisling's cooking for a week and then my trip to Lourdes with

116

Antonia is hijacked by that compulsive chatterbox of a bookseller—and you call it a little inconvenience!"

Aisling grinned and turned her attention back to the situation outside. "What happened to the two gorillas?" she asked Deirdre.

"John and Perry knocked them out and Perry's just finished bringing them into the house. I must say he surprised me; I didn't think he'd be that effective."

Aisling didn't like the admiring look in Deirdre's eyes. "I wish John Smith would hurry up," she said. "I don't trust Peregrine in there with him. Maybe we should go back in and see if he needs help."

Just then, John Smith and Peregrine came out of the house. John Smith carefully shut the front door behind him and climbed into the ambulance.

"Great to have you back with us again, Florence," he said. "Are you all right?"

Florence smiled bravely. "Perfectly, dear boy."

"She's not," Aisling said. "What did that creep Shavitov do to you?"

"I'm just a little shaken, that's all. And Shavitov's not so bad, Aisling. He was telling me all about his very sad youth: it's no wonder he's turned out as he has. And I'm sure Lerntowski is a bad influence on him."

Aisling grinned at Peter behind Florence's back. Trust her to find something good even in someone as rotten as Shavitov.

"Why was the bounder holding you prisoner?" Peregrine asked.

Aisling looked at him coldly. "You know why. They were hoping to lure Seamus to Lourdes and trap him

117

too. It nearly worked. If it hadn't been for John Smith..."

"Yes, indeed," Florence said warmly. "It was very kind of you, John, to come to my rescue."

John Smith grinned. "All part of the service. Now, if we're finished with the social chitchat, I suggest we leave. It should take our three friends some time to get out of that cellar and, by then, I hope to be well on the way home."

"We can't go home!" Florence, Deirdre and Peregrine all said together.

"You sound like the chorus line in a musical. Drive on, Deirdre, we'll talk about it on the way. Now, what exactly is your problem?"

"We absolutely must find the nuclear waste flasks," Peregrine said, "before anyone discovers they're missing. Can you imagine the trouble there'll be if one of those left-wing newspapers or ITV (or even the BBC, damn them) gets wind of it? It will be frightfully difficult to hush up."

"Just as well," said Deirdre. "The bigger the scandal, the better."

"I think you're both forgetting the main point," Florence suggested quietly from the back of the ambulance. "These things are lethal. If what that poor deluded man Shavitov told me is true, S.K.U.N.K. intend to plant the flasks they've stolen in some of the world's main cities. They will then threaten to explode them if they don't get what they want. Even you must admit, Seamus, we cannot allow that."

"Hmph," Seamus grunted. "I suppose you're right. Though you do realise that I'd been looking forward to my first holiday in over thirty years?"

"Tough," Aisling muttered under her breath.

Peter grinned.

John Smith sighed. "I think the stolen flasks are in Spain. Probably in Galicia. I had hoped to send you all back to Ireland and get down there myself, to see what I can do, but if you insist on coming with me, I suppose we'd better get this overcrowded vehicle of mercy on the road south. Head for the centre of town, Deirdre: we'll find directions there."

"And the first thing we shall do is stop for a nice cup of tea," Florence said firmly. "And a decent meal. I'm sure you young things haven't been eating properly."

John Smith turned round with a warm smile. "Thank goodness we have you with us now, Flo, to look after us. I was quite worried about you for a time, there."

"Hmph, yes." Seamus grunted from the back of the ambulance. "It's good to see you safe and well, Florence. I've..."

"Yes?"

"I've missed you," Seamus growled awkwardly.

"And I've missed you, too, Seamus. And even Mulligan here. He looks hungry, Aisling. I hope you've been feeding him?"

"He saved us from Shavitov again," Aisling said. "As soon as we find some food, I intend to give him as much as he can eat. He definitely deserves it."

13

Sightseeing

They stopped at the Restaurant Sainte Bernadette in a narrow side-street near the centre
of Lourdes. Even Florence found the meal delicious: *soupe
du jour* followed by fresh trout from the river Gave, and
finally a delicious melt-in-the-mouth pastry and a
selection of French cheese. The proprietress piled a plate
high with tasty scraps for Mulligan. He wound round
her ankles like a short furry snake, purring his gratitude,
and gave the others a filthy look as if to say "at least
somebody around here loves me. You lot should be
reported to the ISPCA." Then he fell on the food as if he
hadn't eaten for about three years.

"*Il est mignon, le chat,*" the proprietress said
approvingly. "He is very sweet."

Seamus had stayed in the ambulance. When Aisling
brought him out his meal on a tray, she found him sitting
up in bed, drawing a map of Spain. She looked at all the
roads and towns marked in neatly. "Did you do all that
without an atlas?" she asked, amazed.

"We are not all as ignorant as you," Seamus snorted.
"In my day, we were taught geography properly."

Aisling decided to ignore this. She pointed to the map.
"Galicia's in the top left-hand corner there, isn't it?" she

120

asked.

"Top left-hand corner! I take it you mean the north-west?"

"Whatever. How far away do you think it is?"

"Far enough," Seamus grunted. "And the sooner we get started the better. So tell the rest of them, if they want to go on this madcap adventure, to get a move on."

"Don't you want to stop S.K.U.N.K?"

"I wanted a holiday." Seamus complained peevishly. "But obviously nobody cares a toss about what I want."

He was still sulking when they came back to the ambulance after lunch. This time John Smith drove. They passed the basilica at the centre of Lourdes. The space in front of it was big enough to hold at least five hockey pitches, Aisling thought, and it was filled with tourists and pilgrims. She wondered if Antonia Browne was there with her flock of aged and infirm.

A few minutes later, she had an answer. They had just turned into a long avenue called the Avenue d'Espagne when she noticed a minibus, exactly like the one they'd come in from the airport, parked beside a telephone box. Squeezed into the box, like a stuffed toy in a container too small for it, was...Aisling looked again. It was Antonia Browne!

Miss Browne saw her at exactly the same moment. She stared, her mouth hanging open.

"That was the Browne Cow!" Aisling gasped. "And she's seen us. She'll know where we're going!"

"I would advise you to keep a civil tongue in your head, child," Seamus muttered from the back of the ambulance. "If Antonia's there, I suggest we stop and go back. I owe her an explanation."

"Who's Antonia?" Florence asked.

"A S.K.U.N.K. agent," Aisling said.

"A member of St Philomena's Society for the... ahem. She came to look after me when you were gadding about at Sellafield 'doing your own thing,'" (Seamus made it sound as if she'd been out mugging old-age pensioners) "and was very good to me. Not like some people I know."

"Ah," Florence said. "I thought Aisling and her mother were looking after you."

"Miss Browne took over," Aisling explained. "We couldn't stop her."

"Well?" Seamus asked John Smith. "Are you going to turn round or not? I thought I told you I wanted to speak to Antonia."

"Sorry, grandad. I'd love to facilitate (from the Latin *facere*, Aisling, to make or do; meaning, therefore, 'to make easier') your love-life. I mean, anyone of your advanced age who is still chasing a woman deserves every bit of help he can get."

Seamus muttered something practically unintelligible but Aisling made out the words "cheeky young whippersnapper" and grinned. "However," John Smith continued cheerily, "we must plough on, as the poet said. S.K.U.N.K. is intending to spread fire and radiation (the modern answer to fire and the sword, Aisling: check your *1066 And All That*), and we can't really let them get away with it."

"Won't Antonia warn Lerntowski, now that she's seen where we're headed?" Aisling asked worriedly. "He'll be waiting for us."

"I thought you said Shavitov and Antonia were hoping that Lerntowski wouldn't find out about them," Peter reminded her. "Surely she's unlikely to get in touch with him, even now?"

"She might be desperate. After all, Shavitov's just disappeared, as far as she's concerned."

"I suggest we concentrate on getting to Galicia as fast as we can," John Smith said firmly, "and worry about Miss Browne and Lerntowski later." He switched on the siren in order to roar past an articulated lorry. "Our friend Antonia should be tied up with her religious tour, anyway, and I wouldn't bet on her chances if she tried to interest her flock in a trip to Santiago de Compostela (even though it's a much older religious site) when they've paid for a pilgrimage to Lourdes. There's nothing more dangerous than pilgrims who feel they've been done out of their money's worth."

"There is no need to be anti-religious," Florence sniffed from the back of the ambulance. "I'm surprised at you, John."

"Sorry." He didn't sound it. "Now, why don't you all sit back and enjoy the drive? I can't say I'm as good a tour guide as our Antonia, but I'll do my best."

Aisling groaned. It was bad enough, seven of them being crammed into an ambulance for a journey that looked as if it would take hours, if not days; having to listen to John Smith going on about all the places they were going to pass through would be worse than a double period of geography with Mr Langran. She imagined the headlines in the *Irish Times*: *Ambulance found abandoned in northern Spain: Police say passengers died of boredom.*

☐

They soon left Lourdes behind and climbed higher and higher into the mountains. The road passed through breathtakingly beautiful valleys, alongside icy grey streams and up to where the snow still hadn't melted, despite the warm spring sunshine. As they climbed through forests of tall trees towards the glittering high peaks in the distance, Aisling was reminded of the time they had chased S.K.U.N.K. to Switzerland and she'd been captured by Shavitov and Lerntowski. She crossed her fingers and hoped that Shavitov would stay locked up until he was found by the French police and that they wouldn't need to meet Lerntowski at all.

She had to take it in turns with Peter to sit in the front of the ambulance while Deirdre swapped places with Peregrine. Peregrine was dead boring. Every mountain peak they saw reminded him of something that had happened to him in the Alps or the Hindu Kush, and every bit of snow they passed at the side of the road reminded him of skiing in St Moritz or Gstaad. She wished he'd shut up or fall out of the cab or something. He was such a wally, he might even have been speaking the truth when he'd claimed to be a member of whatever I-love-nuclear-power society he'd said he belonged to. Not even S.K.U.N.K. would be desperate enough to recruit someone like him.

In the late afternoon, they crossed the border and came to the village of Roncesvalles.

"I take it you've heard of Roland?" John Smith asked Aisling.

"No. And I don't want to."

"Is that any way to expand your knowledge? As I don't have a copy of the *Encyclopedia for the Expansion of Young Minds* on me just at the moment (due to circumstances beyond my control), I shall enlighten you. Roland was a French knight who had been left to guard the rear of Charlemagne's army (you do know who Charlemagne was? No? Fortunately, it's not very important for the story). Anyway, Charlemagne and his army had just won a battle against the Moors in Spain and were off home over the Pyrenees. But the Moors, having some sort of religious objection to people who attempted to wipe them out, followed Charlemagne's lot and fell upon the rearguard which was led, as you'll remember if you were paying attention, by our friend Roland."

Aisling groaned.

"Fascinating, isn't it? Anyway, Roland was one of these knights who couldn't bear to ask for help. His men begged him to blow his horn and bring back Charlie and the rest of the army to help them, but oh no, that wasn't the way our Roland did things. So by the time Charlie twigged what was happening and came back to slaughter the infidels (non-Christians, Aisling), old Roland and most of his men were well and truly dead. So they turned him into a great hero and Roncesvalles, where it all happened, became world-famous. It's a funny old life."

"Why don't we stop here for afternoon tea," Florence suggested.

Aisling felt she couldn't bear any more history lessons. And John Smith would be bound to tell her the whole history of Charlemagne, Moorish Spain and anything else he could think of if they stayed there for any time at all. "Aren't we supposed to be in a hurry?" she asked.

Florence put down her knitting. "If you didn't want to stop, you should have asked John Smith to install cooking facilities in this vehicle," she said reprovingly. "Even I am incapable of preparing afternoon tea with nothing but some oxygen equipment and a first-aid kit."

John Smith grinned. "Sorry about that, Florence my love. It was very careless of me. I should have thought."

"You can't think of everything," Florence conceded kindly, "and I've no doubt you had other things on your mind."

"All the same, Aisling has a point. I think we should press on. We'll stop later, if you don't mind."

Florence pursed her lips but didn't argue.

☐

The sun was beginning to set and the shadows lengthen as they reached the town of Pamplona. Peter and Peregrine were lying on the floor in the back of the ambulance, both fast asleep; Seamus was still sketching away and Florence had knitted another side to her jumper. Deirdre was leaning up against the window of the cab with her eyes closed, and Aisling, too, found it difficult to keep awake. John Smith seemed to have no such difficulty.

"Ah, Pamplona!" he announced as they passed a road-sign signalling the start of the town. "Home of the *corrida* where young lads run before the bulls to try to prove they're men. I assume you're too young to have heard of Ernest Hemingway, Aisling?"

"*For Whom the Bell Tolls*," Aisling informed him wearily. "*The Old Man and the Sea; The Sun Also Rises...*"

"My goodness. You never cease to amaze me."

"Rats," Aisling muttered. "Double, triple and quadruple rats. How far is it to wherever we're going?" she asked out loud. "I don't think I'm going to be able to stand it."

"To Galicia? About another couple of hundred miles."

Aisling groaned.

"However," John Smith took his foot off the accelerator and slowed down. "That we shall leave for another day. I think we had better, in deference to our golden oldies, spend the night here. Pamplona, I believe, used to have four hospitals (or hostels, Aisling: hospital, hostel and hotel all come from the same Latin root, as I'm sure you're aware) for pilgrims to stay in on their way to Santiago, but I suppose we'd better look for an inn."

"Make sure it's got no fleas," Seamus grunted from the back of the ambulance.

"Yes, Miranda," John Smith answered primly.

Peter had woken up. "Who's Miranda?" he asked.

"They're just playing word games, again," Aisling explained glumly. "There's a poem called 'Tarantella' by Hilaire Belloc which we had to recite when I was about eight and a half. It begins with 'Do you remember an inn, Miranda?' and then goes on about 'the fleas that tease in the high Pyrenees'."

"'And the wine that tasted of the tar,'" Peregrine added, to Aisling's disgust. "I wouldn't mind a *bota* of wine right now, I must say. It reminds me of the time..."

"What's a *bota*?" Deirdre asked quickly. She must be as fed up with him as I am, Aisling thought.

"Every good ambulance should have an encyclopedia," John Smith maintained. "However, as this one is singularly lacking in reference material, I'll have to explain it to you. Listen carefully children: a *bota* is a sort of leather bottle in which you carry your wine around when you're herding your sheep or goats. It's made of goatskin and lined with tar to make it waterproof. Hence, 'the wine that tasted of the tar.' Any questions?"

"Yes," Aisling muttered under her breath. "Why don't you and Peregrine go off together somewhere and bore yourselves to death?"

She breathed a sigh of relief when they finally stopped outside the Albergo de los Torros. John Smith and Peregrine carried Seamus upstairs to a comfortable bedroom and then they all had a fantastic dinner of soup and Spanish omelette (which seemed to have everything in it but the kitchen sink) followed by creme caramel (which the menu called *flan*). Despite the good food, Aisling found herself practically falling asleep. As soon as the meal was over, she took Mulligan upstairs and crawled into bed.

□

When Aisling opened her eyes, bright morning light streamed in through the slats in the shutters of her window and slanted across her bed. Pushing back the shutters, she looked out over the wavy terracotta slates on the steep roof opposite to the snow-capped Pyrenees beyond. In the distance a donkey brayed. That must be what had woken her.

She looked at her watch: 8 a.m. They'd arranged to meet for breakfast at nine, so she had time to go out and explore. After all, she'd never been in Spain before and, at the rate John Smith was rushing them across the country, if she didn't go out and see it now, she never would. Mulligan had been sleeping in his favourite place, his body under the duvet and his whiskery face snuggled under her chin. She shoved him aside and got up. He growled in annoyance, yawned and went back to sleep. "Honest, Mulligan. You are the laziest cat I know. If it wasn't that I'm scared you might pick up rabies or something, I'd force you to come for a walk with me."

Mulligan opened one eye, stared at her for a second, and then closed it again. She left him there and went out.

She wandered up and down the narrow streets, savouring the sights and smells: the wrinkled, sunburnt old ladies dressed in black; the occasional donkey cart; dark young men who made kissing noises at her as she passed; wizened old men wearing flat caps or Basque berets; houses leaning up against each other higgledy-piggledy, with white-washed walls and tiled roofs; shops, cafés...*Aisling Daly, intrepid explorer, gathers material for her next book on Spain*. It was quite different from France or Switzerland and totally different from Iceland. Maybe she ought to be grateful to S.K.U.N.K. for giving her so many chances to travel!

The cafés were open and full of men drinking coffee and eating funny-looking pastries or rolls. She began to

feel hungry herself. She turned back towards the centre
of town, hoping she would be able to find her way back
to the hotel.

She had to wait for a minibus to pass before she could
cross a busy street. It braked suddenly and she found
herself face to face with the driver. She wished the ground
would open up and swallow her: the bloated face with
small evil eyes which stared back at her, full of hate,
belonged to...Shavitov! For a minute she felt paralysed.
Then she started to run. The minibus followed her. She
turned down a side-street. It got even closer. She looked
for an alleyway too narrow for the bus to come down, but
there wasn't one and the street was deserted, there was
nobody she could ask for help. She ran on, waiting for
the minibus to run her down. *Irish schoolgirl victim of
hit-and-run driver in Pamplona!* Whatever would her
parents say?

She risked a glance over her shoulder and her foot
hit an uneven paving-stone, sending her sprawling.

She heard the bus stop as she started to struggle to
her feet. A fat pink hand grabbed her arm and held it
tightly. Miss Browne pulled her up. "Why, chicken, there's
no need to be scared. We're only wanting to give you a
lift back to your godfather."

"I can manage, thanks," Aisling said hopefully, trying
to pull her arm away.

Miss Browne held on firmly. "Not at all, pet. You
might have hurt your foot there. Come on, let me help
you into the bus."

14
Kidnapped

Antonia Browne pushed Aisling up the steps of the minibus and shut the door behind them. The bus was full of the elderly ladies who had been with Miss Browne the day before, when they'd chased the ambulance through the streets of Lourdes. "Help me!" Aisling appealed to them. "She wants to kidnap me!"

Miss Browne shook her head reprovingly, fluttering her many chins. "We mustn't be so melodramatic, pet, now must we? Just tell me where Seamus is and Teddybear will take you back to him."

"When are we leaving for Lourdes?" the lady with the blue rinse demanded. "You promised us last night that we would go back there first thing this morning. The others in the party will be worrying about us."

"I'm worrying about Kathleen," another lady said plaintively.

Miss Browne's fat cheeks creased in an oily smile. "Of course, chickens. Don't distress yourselves." She turned to Aisling. "Now, pet, where are your godfather and Florence?"

Aisling thought quickly. "In Lourdes," she said, looking Miss Browne straight in the eye. "I came down here with Deirdre and Peregrine and Peter. We wanted to see the bull-running."

"Zees ees a lie!" shouted Shavitov from the driver's seat. "Do not believes her. She ees alvays telling ze lies."

The elderly ladies flinched.

"It's true," Aisling insisted. "Seamus wanted to visit Lourdes. You know that. He wanted to be with you." Had she gone too far? she wondered.

Apparently not. Miss Browne blushed and patted her hair. She turned to Shavitov, "Well, Teddybear, it does sound as if we've made a mistake. Perhaps we should go back to Lourdes after all?"

"She ees telling ze lies!" Shavitov screeched. He squeezed his vast bulk out of the driver's seat and stood up. "You are foolish vomunn, no? You believes everyzink she says. I, Shavitov, hav vays of making her talk."

"Ooooh!" went all the elderly ladies faintly.

"Don't you lay a hand on that child, you monster!" threatened the one with the blue rinse. Aisling wondered if she'd been a headmistress before she retired, or a hospital matron: she sounded bossy enough for either. But Shavitov was unimpressed. Nobody, Aisling thought with a shudder, except perhaps Lerntowski, could stop Shavitov from doing anything he wanted to, including tearing her limb from limb. She wished she'd brought Mulligan with her; no, she wished she'd stayed in bed with him at the hotel or never left Ireland in the first place. But wishes weren't going to help now...

Miss Browne frowned. "We'll have none of that, Teddybear," she said, reprovingly.

Shavitov, to Aisling's amazement, blushed and sat down again, like a little child who's been told off. He glared at Aisling behind Miss Browne's back: if looks could kill, she'd have been pulverised into a tiny pile of dust. She drew closer to Miss Browne. She'd never thought she'd end up viewing the Browne Cow as a protector and she wondered how long it would last.

"I knows Seamus is here," Shavitov muttered. "I can smells heem. He vill be going to La Coruña to try to put, how you say? ze spanner in ze spokes, yes?"

Miss Browne looked surprised. "Why would he do that, Teddybear? Why would he want to go to La Coruña?"

Shavitov smiled shiftily. "Did I say La Coruña, yes?" he asked. "I means Santiago. He goes to Santiago to be ze peelgreem. I zeenks ve should be ze peelgreems too, no?"

"No!" said Blue Rinse firmly from the back of the bus.

"You shuts up!" Shavitov yelled at her. He turned back to Antonia. "Ve takes ze ladies on ze peelgreemage to Santiago, no? Zay likes zees more zan Lourdes."

"Well, I don't know, pet...."

"You tells zem." Shavitov put the bus into gear.

"Let me off!" Aisling pleaded with Antonia as the minibus began to move. "Deirdre and Peregrine will be looking for me."

"We want to go back to Lourdes!" the elderly ladies complained, like a cackle of hens.

Miss Browne glanced at Shavitov's set face. "I'm sorry, chickens. It looks as if we're all going to Santiago." She forced a smile. "I think you will enjoy this trip. Santiago de Compostela is a much, much older place of pilgrimage than Lourdes: people were going there from all over the world as far back as the ninth century. It was more

famous than the pilgrim road to Canterbury and almost
as popular as a pilgrimage to the Holy Land. Those who
travelled to the shrine of Saint James (Iago, in Spanish,
hence Santiago) believed they would shorten their time
in purgatory and be forgiven for their sins...."

Aisling closed her mind to Antonia's boring monologue.
What was she going to do? She glanced at her watch. It
was after nine: the others would be up now and wondering
what had happened to her. She wondered if there was
any way she could leave them a sign. She thought of the
babes in the wood and the crumbs of bread they left
behind to mark the path back to their cottage. And then
there were all the adventure stories she'd read where
people dropped their handkerchiefs or their scarves or
whatever along the way to show where they'd been taken.
She felt in her pockets. All she had were paper tissues.
She could try dropping one of her runners out of the
window and the other one further on, but the chance of
John Smith and the others seeing either of them was
minuscule and she'd be less well able to escape (assuming she ever got the chance), if she was barefoot.

Rats and quintuple rats. Like Miss Browne's ladies,
she was stuck until they got to...where? Shavitov had
said La Coruña. She tried to visualise the sketch map
Seamus had been drawing in the ambulance, but all she
could remember was the vague outline of a straight
coastline running across the page and turning south at
the left-hand edge. North-west edge, she corrected herself
with a wry smile. Maybe Mr Langran was right and she
should concentrate more in geography: *Irish student wins
National Geographic Society's Gold Medal!* She only hoped

she'd get home again safely to give it a try.

□

They sped across the flat plain of northern Spain. The elderly ladies, like Aisling, had given up complaining and most of them had fallen asleep. Aisling dozed too, half-waking now and again to hear Miss Browne burbling on about Moors and Christians, cathedrals and monasteries or even, once, a magic cock and a hen which came alive on the dinner table after they'd been roasted, to prove the innocence of a young lad wrongly convicted of theft. She was aware of towns with narrow medieval streets, white-washed villages and, most of all, endless vistas of brown earth patterned by rows and rows of stumpy, leafless vines.

They stopped in Leon for lunch, Shavitov parking the minibus in yet another medieval square opposite another huge Gothic cathedral. If they really were on a pilgrimage, Aisling thought, they would have had plenty of opportunities to pray. And prayer was definitely something she could do with now; nothing else was going to save her from Antonia and Shavitov, who stuck to her like two fat leeches. She was hemmed in between them at the table in the restaurant where they ate and even when she went to the toilet Antonia insisted on coming with her, checking that there wasn't a window she could escape through, and standing outside the door until she came out again.

The ladies seemed to have been cowed into accepting their fate, although Blue Rinse still muttered about

complaining to the tour company when they got back to
Ireland and suing St Philomena's Society for misrepres-
entation. After lunch, Antonia Browne suggested they
have a look round the cathedral, "which is in the purest
Gothic style to be found in Spain, chickens. It was built
in the thirteenth century, almost as a lesson in the new
architecture. When you're inside, just look at the way
the whole cathedral is flooded with light from these
marvellous windows: quite different from the narrow
windows of the earlier Romanesque churches."

"I'll come with you," Aisling volunteered. "I just love
Gothic architecture."

"You come back to the bus with us, pet. We'll wait for
the others there." Miss Browne's hand hadn't left her
arm and Shavitov hadn't left her side.

"All right," Aisling said meekly. She turned as if she
was going to go with them quietly, then pulled her arm
quickly away from Miss Browne and tried to dash across
the square.

Shavitov's hand fell on her shoulder like a concrete
block. "So? You zeenks you can run avay, yes? You zeenks
ve arre stupid, yes? Eet ees you zat ees ze stupid leetle
girrl." He dragged her back to the minibus.

"Ouch!" gasped Aisling. "You're hurting me. Let me
go!"

She appealed to the elderly ladies, especially Blue
Rinse. They just smiled embarrassedly and went off
towards the cathedral. Now I know what it must have
felt like to be a Jew in Hitler's Germany, Aisling thought
bitterly, as Shavitov threw her back into her seat and
Miss Browne plonked herself down beside her, hemming

her in once more: nobody cares.

She stared at the huge wooden doors and heavily decorated stone arch at the entrance to the cathedral, waiting for the little old ladies to come out again. Maybe they would get help when they were in there? Maybe they'd find a policeman?

She jumped as Shavitov started the motor. "Ve goes now, yes?"

"But, Teddybear, we have to wait for my ladies."

"Why? Zey arre nuisance. Ve leeves zem here, yes?"

"Oh no." Miss Browne sounded distressed. "We can't do that. I am responsible for them. It's one thing, giving them a different tour, although I think they're beginning to appreciate how much more interesting this one is and, after all, they're getting a marvellous chance to travel at no extra cost. But I can't just abandon them, Teddybear. We have promised to take them to Saint James's tomb in Santiago, and take them we shall."

Shavitov looked as if he was going to argue, then he sulkily shut off the engine again. Aisling went back to watching the cathedral. Her heart sank as the ladies all trooped out again, twittering together like a flock of starlings: they weren't going to be any help at all. Blue Rinse sat down directly behind her. She ignored Antonia's disapproving stare. "Are you all right, dear?" she asked.

"Why didn't you tell someone?" Aisling asked quickly as Shavitov drove off.

"Tell them what, chicken?" Miss Browne smiled. "That ve're on a pilgrimage to Santiago? Why would anyone want to know that?"

Aisling looked desperately back at Blue Rinse. "You

137

know what I mean. The police."

Blue Rinse sighed and looked sad. "Miss Browne is right, dear. I mean, who would believe me?"

Aisling's heart sank. "Why did you come back to the bus then?"

Miss Browne frowned. "Shh, now, pet. That's no question to ask." She glared at Blue Rinse, threateningly.

Blue Rinse continued to ignore her. "Everything on this tour is paid for in advance," she explained apologetically. "And none of us is rich. We only brought a little pocket-money each to buy souvenirs. We don't have the money to get back to Ireland, or even to return to France. So what can we do?"

Miss Browne smiled in satisfaction. "Don't you worry, love. We'll enjoy the pilgrimage and then get you all back to Ireland safe and sound. Teddybear may sound gruff at times," her voice sank to a whisper, "but underneath, he has a heart of gold. He really wants you all to have a good time."

If she believed that, she'd believe anything, Aisling thought bitterly. An idea struck her: maybe Miss Browne didn't know about S.K.U.N.K.? Maybe she was just in love with Shavitov? Once she learnt the truth, she might help them all escape!

"You do know that he's with this evil organisation called S.K.U.N.K., don't you?" she asked. "They're a gang of thugs with some sort of Central-European name. Seamus says the letters stand for skulduggery, killing, unscrupulousness, nastiness and corruption, so you can see how awful they are. And right now they're holding the world to ransom again."

Miss Browne looked down at her with a patronising smile. "Children really do have such incredible imaginations. We shouldn't let it run away with us now, should we, chicken."

"But it's the truth! I *know*. We were up against Shavitov in Switzerland, when S.K.U.N.K. tried to blow a hole in the ozone layer; and again in Iceland when they tried to split the world apart. Now they've stolen a whole shipload of spent nuclear fuel flasks and they're threatening to open them and contaminate the world! We have to stop them!"

"Really, chicken. That's quite enough."

Aisling turned round to Blue Rinse. "You believe me, don't you?"

Blue Rinse looked embarrassed. "Yes, dear," she said, but she didn't sound convinced. "I think maybe you're over-tired. Perhaps you should try and get some more sleep."

Aisling sighed and turned to stare gloomily out of the window. She'd tried everything. All she could do now was wait.

15
Santiago de Compostela

T he countryside changed as they travelled
further west. The road wound upwards into a
landscape which could have been the West of Ireland,
with stone everywhere: in the walls around the tiny fields,
in the houses, in wayside churches, in the tiny little
barns sitting on pillars of granite (which Miss Browne
informed them were called *horreos*), and cropping up
through the grass and gorse of the fields themselves. If
only, Aisling thought, she was in the car with her family
heading for Connemara, instead of in this minibus with
Shavitov and Miss Browne, heading goodness knows
where: *Promising young Irish hockey-player last seen in
minibus in north-west Spain. Aisling Daly was apparently
travelling with the group of elderly Irish pilgrims who
disappeared from Lourdes yesterday in mysterious
circumstances.*

It was late afternoon by the time they finally arrived
in Santiago. The town was full of tourists and Shavitov's
temper wasn't improved by having to drive slowly through
the narrow crowded streets. "Vat for you vanted to come
to Santiago for?" he grumbled. "I says ve go to La Coruña,
but you knows better, yes?"

"I promised our ladies to take them to the shrine of

Saint James, Teddybear," Antonia replied. "They are, after all, on a pilgrimage."

Aisling cursed the fact that the bus was airconditioned: she couldn't even pull down a window and cry for help. She tried looking appealingly at the tourists crammed up against them and mouthing "help!" but very few even noticed her and those who did looked away quickly in embarrassment. It was hopeless.

Finally they stopped in a square in front of a huge cathedral, decorated like a crazy wedding cake. Miss Browne had her guide book out again. "Just look at that magnificent archway, chickens, on the west front," she commanded her ladies. "It's called *El Portico de la Gloria*, the gate of glory, and it is, as you can see, absolutely magnificent. When you go over, do study the figures properly: like our own Irish stone crosses, each section of carving tells a story. And when you get inside, you'll be amazed at the size of the nave, but remember, this cathedral was built to hold hundreds of pilgrims and was one of the most important churches in Christendom. The remains of the holy apostle are kept in a silver urn in the crypt. I suggest you pay a quick visit to it now, maybe say a little prayer, and then we'll come back tomorrow and do the cathedral properly."

The elderly ladies, like elderly sheep, Aisling thought, got out and trotted obediently across the square to the cathedral.

"Now ve leaves them, no?" Shavitov said hopefully.

"No, dearest. We can't do that. It was a bit naughty of us to take them to Spain when they wanted to go to Lourdes and we can't just abandon them here. I mean,

I have already...er, misplaced dear Seamus and the other members of the tour: I only hope they are all all right."

So do I, Aisling muttered to herself.

"Lerntowski vill not likes ze old ladies, no," Shavitov stated.

Aisling shivered at the mention of Lerntowski's name. "I thought he wasn't supposed to know where you two were," she said without thinking.

Shavitov whirled round to glare at her. "Vat does you knows, leetle girl? You theenks you knows more than Shavitov, yes?"

"It's all right, Teddybear. Leave her alone. It was you yourself who said we had to keep our love a secret from your friend, though I still can't see why."

"Zees orrible peoples vat treecked me, Shavitov, in Lourdes—ze Grandaddy and zat John Smith and ze ozers: I must varn Lerntowski zat zey arre in Spain."

"Do you mean Seamus? But surely we left him in France? I mean, when I came round that corner in Lourdes and saw you bursting out of that house, Teddybear..."

"Yes," Aisling said. "I was wondering how you'd escaped."

Shavitov turned to glare at her again. "You zought you had me, Shavitov, locked up, yes? But you zeenks Shavitov ees baby, no? Shavitov has ze arms of steel." He flexed his powerful muscles. "For me to breaks down leetle door, ees no troubles. And my lovely Antonia, she passes by outside viz her bus." He gazed at Miss Browne like a dewy-eyed puppy. Aisling thought she was going to be sick. "But now, ve must go. Eef zees orrible leetle girrl ees in Spain, zen her grandaddy and John Smith arre in Spain also. Lerntowski must be varned," he repeated.

Aisling thought quickly. "I need to go to the toilet," she told Antonia.

"Oh dear, chicken. Can't we wait?"

"No."

"She does not needs to go nowhere," Shavitov growled threateningly. "She stays in bus, yes? Ve does not vants her to run away. Ven ve finds her grandaddy, she ees useful to us, no?"

Miss Browne wagged a plump finger at him. "Really, Teddybear, you must learn to be more considerate. If the poor child needs to go to the toilet, then we must find her a toilet. You wait here until I come back."

"She stays in bus." Shavitov thumped his huge hand on the steering wheel. Aisling flinched.

Miss Browne appeared unperturbed. "Now, now, Teddybear, what did I just say? You really must control your temper. Take a deep breath and count to ten, now, like a good boy. We won't be a minute." She stood up determinedly.

Shavitov looked like a gorilla who'd been asked to work out the theory of relativity: Aisling felt she could almost see the thoughts crawling across his brain like a progression of very tired slugs. He scratched his head slowly. "Okays," he said at last. "But me, Shavitov, I comes too."

Miss Browne sighed. "Very well then, Teddybear. If you insist."

She led Aisling across the square while Shavitov

trundled along behind, much more like a huge grizzly than a teddy bear. Aisling realised she'd never be able to cuddle a teddy bear again. They pushed their way through the dense crowd. Aisling heard snippets of various languages: English, American, French, German, Swedish, Japanese...She thought of trying again to appeal for help, but she knew what would happen: nobody would believe her. She'd have to help herself.

She waited until Shavitov was separated from them by a group of nuns. "Look over there!" she said urgently to Miss Browne. "Isn't that the Pope?" Miss Browne spun round, letting go of Aisling's arm. Aisling ran. She dodged in and out of the people in the square and dived down a street at the other side. Footsteps pounded behind her: Shavitov must be on her tail. She raced down narrow streets, up flights of stone steps, across squares, round fountains, until she finally found herself in the middle of a street market. She glanced over her shoulder: Shavitov was still behind her. He was panting in loud gasps, like an asthmatic in a heatwave, but the gap between them was slowly narrowing.

She ran between rows of stalls laden with fruit. Passing another fountain, she found herself faced with more stalls, this time piled high with fish and smelling of the sea. She had a pain in her side and breathing was becoming more and more difficult. And she'd always thought she was reasonably fit! If she survived this, she promised herself, she would definitely take hockey training more seriously next year.

Suddenly, there was a yell from behind her. Then came a tremendous crash. She looked round: Shavitov was lying across the ruins of a fish stall in a pile of cod. As she watched, he struggled to his feet, but was stopped by an uncontrollable fit of sneezing. She couldn't believe her eyes when a huge orange cat, the tail of a fish hanging out of one side of his mouth, its head out of the other, disentangled himself from the wreckage of the stall and trotted towards her, his orange tail bushed out and sticking up straight behind him. It was Mulligan! She picked him up and hugged him tightly, ignoring the fish squashed up against her jumper.

Then Peter appeared, dodging out of the way of the irate stallholder. "*Schnell*, Ash!" he shouted. "Quick! This way!"

Feeling as if her lungs were going to burst (and not just because of the ghastly smell of fish coming from Mulligan), she followed him. The ambulance was parked at the far side of the square. They scrambled in, Florence shut the door, John Smith crashed the gears into first, flicked the switch to activate the siren and they roared off, people leaping out of their way as they passed. Shavitov, his eyes running, sneezes bursting out of him like a twenty-one gun salute, followed them for a few yards and then gave up. He watched them drive out of the square, his mouth working, his clenched fist raised in the air.

"Well, well, well. The wanderer has returned." Aisling never would have thought she'd be so pleased to hear Seamus's grumpy voice. "Perhaps you'd care to tell us why you caused us so much trouble in Pamplona. Not to mention why you've allowed that ill-mannered feline to bring his malodorous fishy supper in here."

"I was kidnapped by Shavitov and Antonia Browne. I could have been killed!"

"You held us up," Seamus complained. "Florence insisted that we waste hours searching high and low for you. I thought you realised that this was a serious mission? If the world is contaminated by radiation just because you decided to go sightseeing..."

"Did they look after you all right, child?" Florence at least was concerned. "Have you eaten properly?"

"What happened to you?" Peter asked. "How did you get to Santiago? And why was Shavitov following you?"

"Shavitov here?" John Smith appeared to hear the name for the first time and raised an eyebrow. "I thought we'd left him safely trussed up in France."

"Well you didn't," Aisling said. "He managed to smash his way out of that room you locked him into and I gather Antonia Browne just happened to be passing with her minibus of pilgrims as he came out of the house. So they've kidnapped the whole lot of them and dragged them all the way across Spain to here."

"Then Antonia Browne is a member of S.K.U.N.K. after all. I'm sorry I didn't believe you," Peter apologised. He grinned. "I never thought they'd be that desperate."

"Funnily enough, I don't think she knows about S.K.U.N.K.," Aisling said slowly, "though I did try to tell her. It was Shavitov who wanted to come here. She just came along with him because she's in love with him, the silly old cow."

"Aisling!" Seamus exploded. "I'd thank you to mind your language."

"Well, she is," Aisling muttered. And the sooner you

stop being besotted by her, the better, she added to herself. Out loud she said, "Why does Shavitov want to come here? And why are we here too? Is this where S.K.U.N.K. has hidden the nuclear waste thingies?"

John Smith answered her. "The nuclear waste thingies, as you so elegantly put it, Aisling, are, Peregrine thinks, in La Coruña, which is not so very far from here. You've heard of La Coruña, haven't you? Where the Spanish Armada sailed from in 1588?"

"Shavitov mentioned La Coruña," Aisling remembered.

"There you are then. You're very lucky, in fact; we almost decided to bypass Santiago and go straight there, but Peregrine thought he might get more information about what was happening from the *Ayuntamiento*—the town hall—here. In fact, if he hadn't convinced us to try officialdom, and if Peter there hadn't decided to let Mulligan out for a breath of fresh air...."

"I didn't," Peter corrected him. "He escaped. It must have been the smell of all that fish, even from the other side of the square."

"Trust Mulligan. He'd smell food a mile away against the wind."

"Did you find out anything more about where S.K.U.N.K.'s keeping the nuclear waste?" Aisling asked.

"No. The police are combing the coast but it's not easy. It must be somewhere near La Coruña, though. Everything points to that."

Aisling glanced over her shoulder. Peregrine was sitting in the back of the ambulance with his arm round Deirdre. She lowered her voice. "Are you sure Peregrine's not trying to mislead you? If he says they're there, then they obviously must be somewhere else. You know he's with S.K.U.N.K.. He's just trying to send you off on a wild goose chase."

"Here we go, here we go, here we go again," hummed John Smith. "She has a one-track mind, our Aisling. Not everybody on God's earth, you know, belongs to that dastardly organisation; some people find other things to do to pass the time of day."

Aisling didn't answer. They would find out eventually that she was right. In the meantime, it was up to her to keep an eye on Peregrine and make sure he didn't lead them straight into a S.K.U.N.K. trap. She held Mulligan more tightly. He burped a cloud of fishy breath all over her and then struggled out of her arms, jumped over the back of the seat on to Seamus's stomach and started to wash himself.

"Get off, you evil, foul-smelling monstrosity!" Seamus yelled. "You stink worse than the hold of a trawler." Mulligan gave a yelp as he landed on the floor and then slunk, growling, underneath Seamus's bed. Seamus turned to John Smith: "I suggest you curtail this tour of the city and suburbs, fascinating as it may be, and get us out into the country. I still fail to see why we had to come here in the first place."

"I received valuable information from the chief of police here," Peregrine said smugly.

"It's all right, Grandad," John Smith reassured Seamus. "We're nearly out of the city now. Although I feel we haven't done justice to what is, after all, one of the most beautiful cities in Spain, let alone told Aisling all about Saint James who was killed by King Herod, stuck into a marble sepulchre (from the Latin *sepelire*, to bury, Aisling) and put to sea, though not in a beautiful pea-green boat like the owl and the pussycat, I'm afraid." He swung out on to the wrong side of the road to pass a donkey cart. "The saint, or rather his corpse, then sailed all the way to Spain, up the river Ulla and was buried right underneath where the cathedral now stands. As you can imagine, a host of miracles occurred almost immediately and, since then, pilgrims have been flooding here, like housewives to the Christmas sales."

"I know all that," Aisling muttered. "Antonia Browne was full of it."

"But did she tell you that the emblem of the pilgrims was a scallop shell, just like the one Shell Oil uses nowadays? And did you know that the French for scallop is *coquille St Jacques* or shell of Saint James? No, I thought you didn't."

Aisling groaned.

"There you are then. And here we are at the edge of the city, and you've hardly seen any of it. I fear that you'll just have to look it all up in a good encyclopedia when we get home; I only hope our friend Antonia is giving her elderly tourists better value for money."

"Rats," Aisling muttered to herself. "Rats to the power of four hundred."

□

They stopped in a picturesque village to buy hard brown bread, dried-up-looking sausage, a hunk of extremely hard cheese, a bottle of local red wine, some mineral water and a kilo of wizened-looking oranges (over which Florence had haggled with the shop owner) and then picnicked on a hillside in the evening sunshine. For the first time since they'd left home, Aisling found herself enjoying herself. "Wouldn't it be great to be able to forget about S.K.U.N.K. and just have a holiday here?" she asked Peter.

"Mmm," he answered through a mouthful of bread and cheese. "I've always wanted to see Spain, but not from the back of an ambulance."

"I want to go home," Seamus complained. "The sooner we find out where they have this nuclear waste and remove it, the better."

"I absolutely couldn't agree more, Mr O'Toole." Peregrine nodded his head emphatically. "We have wasted far too much time already, actually, and we are really no further on. I only hope that the official powers have had better luck."

"The official powers?" John Smith raised an eyebrow. "When I asked for help from them in France, I was given a polite brush-off. What makes you think they're going to help us now?"

"Ahem." Peregrine looked embarrassed. "I think they hoped, actually, that you would keep S.K.U.N.K. busy in France for a little longer, while they worked on the Spanish end of things. It is absolutely vital that we find the flasks before S.K.U.N.K. moves them out of the country."

"Have you any idea yet in which cities they're going to plant them?" Peter asked.

"Yes. The bounders have threatened the Houses of Parliament in London, the Bundeshaus in Bonn and the Assemblée Nationale in Paris. We absolutely must stop them before they get the flasks there."

"We?" Deirdre asked. "Do you mean 'we' as in 'us here in this ambulance' or 'we' as in the nuclear industry?"

"I've no doubt the nuclear industry will be really delighted to have your assistance if they haven't actually found the flasks themselves yet."

"I'm sure they will." Deirdre sounded bitter.

"However, there's just one slight problem. I'm afraid I'm going to have to ask you all to sign the Official Secrets Act. I brought some copies along in my briefcase, just in case we got this far."

"The *what*?" Aisling thought Seamus was about to explode.

"The Official Secrets Act. It means you swear never to tell anyone about what we find in La Coruña. I'm afraid it's terribly necessary, actually. We can't afford to let the public know that spent nuclear fuel rods have been stolen from Sellafield. You really must see that."

"And if we refuse to sign?" Deirdre asked coldly.

"Why should you? You must realise it's in the national interest that this never gets out."

"Whose national interest?" Deirdre spat at him. "Ireland's? We've been trying to close down Sellafield for years. We don't want your pollution washing up on our shores. And I doubt if the people of Britain are that sold on nuclear power either. You talk of national interest and you mean politics and big business. It's all a con. And once people see how easy it is to steal nuclear

151

waste, and how dangerous the stuff is, they're going to be even more against nuclear power. So you can stuff your official secrets act. Greenpeace is going to blow this thing wide open."

"Good girl, Deirdre. That's the way." Florence was quite excited. She caught Aisling's eye and blushed. "Has everyone had enough to eat?" she asked quickly. "We really should have stopped somewhere and had a properly cooked meal."

"I'd rather like to get the documents signed before we leave, actually," Peregrine said mildly. He went over to the ambulance, pulled his briefcase from under the seat, and took out a sheaf of official-looking forms. "Please read them through carefully to make sure you know what you're swearing to, and then sign on the dotted line at the end. Hold on a minute. I have some pens here too."

"Bless your bureaucratic (from the French *bureau* meaning an office, Aisling) brass buttons, young man. I'll give the nuclear lobby this, you always come prepared. Or maybe you were a boy scout in your youth?"

Peregrine looked down his long nose at John Smith. "Such levity ill-becomes you, Smith. Actually, I would have thought that, with your past service to Her Majesty's Government, I could at least depend on you to back me up."

"I no longer work for the government and I'll back up whom I please. In this particular case, I'm afraid I'm on the side of Deirdre here and good old Florence. We'll do all we can to stop S.K.U.N.K. from carrying out their dastardly plot, but don't expect help in hushing this thing up. Not from any of us."

Peregrine turned to Seamus. "What about you, Mr O'Toole? Do you want to stab the nuclear industry in the back, too?"

"I saw what happened at Hiroshima and Nagasaki," Seamus said quietly. "All experiments with nuclear fission should have stopped after that. The tests which your government, America and France have carried out since then have contaminated the earth, polluted the atmosphere, and led to the deaths of many of those who were involved as well as of innocent fishermen who just happened to be around at the time. And now you're selling the materials to anyone who has the money to pay for them, so every tin-pot dictator can make his own nuclear bomb. And you think that I should be in favour of the nuclear industry?!"

"Nuclear power can be used for peaceful purposes too, Mr O'Toole," Peregrine pointed out stiffly.

"What man has made, man is capable of mucking up: Murphy's first law. Nuclear power is far too dangerous for a race of power-crazy disaster-prone apes to play with. So put that stupid piece of paper away, man, and help Florence pack up. We've wasted enough time here already."

Peregrine sighed. "You leave me no option," he said sadly. "I had hoped this wouldn't be necessary." He drew a gun from his pocket. "All right now, who will be the first to sign."

16

Getting Closer

J ohn Smith didn't seem to be particularly worried about Peregrine's gun. "There you are, Aisling," he said cheerfully. "I told you not everybody belongs to S.K.U.N.K. Though I can't help wondering if some of the people who claim they're fighting on our side are all that much better."

"Look, Smith. I'm terribly sorry about this, old man." Peregrine did sound genuinely sorry. "But I can't let you help us find this waste unless I can be absolutely sure you won't let the public know. You must see it would be terrifically bad for public confidence."

"And how!" Deirdre muttered. "You're a...a skunk, Perry. John's right; you're as bad as them."

Peregrine ran his free hand through his immaculately-combed fair hair. "Look, Deirdre. We *need* nuclear power. I wish I could persuade you that all this bosh about alternative energy sources is just that: pure rubbish. It'll never work. I mean, I'm awfully fond of you. You know that. And I'm sure you're reasonably intelligent for a woman. But you can't really believe in wind and wave power and all that rot. It's just that you've let yourself be led astray by all these long-haired, sandal-wearing, drug-taking, vegetarian hippies in Greenpeace."

"Like myself?" Florence asked sweetly. "Thank you, dear boy."

Peregrine blushed.

"Are you going to stay here arguing all night?" Seamus growled from the back of the ambulance. "In case none of you has noticed, it's getting late. I daresay I can spend the night quite comfortably where I am, and Florence might manage on the other bunk. If the rest of you are going to camp out under the stars, I wish you luck but I'd have thought you'd be more comfortable with a roof over your heads."

"Seamus is quite right." Florence stood up and started to clear away the remains of the picnic. "Now put that thing away like a good boy, Peregrine, and give me a hand."

Peregrine waved the gun at them. "I'm serious," he said seriously. "You have to sign the Official Secrets Act."

"Come on, Perry. Put it away like Florence said and don't be an idiot." Deirdre turned her back on him and began to help Florence to tidy up.

Aisling looked at Peter and stood up too.

Peregrine hesitated. "Please?" he said.

Everyone ignored him. John Smith climbed back into the driver's seat and Peregrine, looking embarrassed, put his pistol away and got into the cab with him. Without a word, Deirdre, Peter and Aisling joined Seamus in the back of the ambulance. Mulligan was there already, sprawled across Seamus's bed, worrying a bit of fishscale out from between the claws of one front paw with his teeth.

Florence packed the remains of the picnic into the

back of the ambulance. She looked at them. "He's quite a nice boy, you know," she said to no one in particular. "You shouldn't judge him too harshly. He's just misguided; I don't think there's really any harm in him."

"He believes in nuclear power and in smothering free speech. Until he changes his mind, I don't want to know him," Deirdre said coldly.

Florence sighed. "Pass me my knitting, then, dear. I think I'll sit in the front for a change."

"Arrogant young pup," Seamus muttered. "Throwing his weight around like that. Trust Florence to take pity on him and leave me with you lot of mindless young idiots and that orange monstrosity there."

Aisling smiled at him. "We love you too, Seamus," she said sweetly.

"Hmph," Seamus snorted.

The ambulance moved off.

They sped along the motorway, following the signs for La Coruña. Aisling, sitting with Peter and Deirdre on the spare bunk, leant back against the side of the ambulance and closed her eyes. It had been a hard day.

She jerked awake as the ambulance slowed to a halt. She'd heard a siren blaring: had she been dreaming, or had Shavitov and Antonia Browne caught up with them again?

She looked through the rear window. They were in a town (she hoped it was La Coruña: she'd done enough travelling through Spain to last her a lifetime), and had stopped in a busy main street. But there was no sign of the minibus behind them. The curtain that separated the cab from the back of the ambulance had been pulled

across: very gently, she pushed it aside to make a gap.
She caught her breath. Just in front of the ambulance,
two men had dismounted from huge black motorbikes
and were now swaggering towards them. They were short
and dark and were dressed in black leather jackets and
jodhpurs. Their heads were covered by evil-looking helmets and their eyes obscured by dark glasses. As they
drew level with the cab, she closed the curtain, picked
Mulligan up from Seamus's bed and hugged him tightly.

Mulligan growled, then started to purr.

"Well? What is it then?" Seamus demanded.

"S.K.U.N.K.'s caught up with us. There are two
horrible men out there, dressed all in black, with motor-
cycle helmets."

"God grant me patience!" Seamus groaned. "That's
not S.K.U.N.K. That's the *guardia civil*." He made it
sound like "gwardeea theeveel."

"The what?"

"The Spanish police," Peter interpreted. "They're very
particular about speeding. Shush a minute and I'll try
and find out what they're saying."

He listened through the curtain and then turned round
to face them. "It's serious," he whispered. "They've had
orders to stop us and take us all to a police station.
Peregrine is looking like...what do you say? The cat who
has caught the mice?"

"I might have guessed," Deirdre said. She stood up.
"Well, I'm not staying here to be arrested. I'm off."

"Where to?" Aisling asked.

"There are some Greenpeace people in La Coruña. I'm
going to find them and get them to help."

157

"We're coming too." Aisling found her holdall and stuffed Mulligan into it. He gave a surprised *prriau*, turned round a couple of times while the bag heaved like a snake digesting a large rat, and then lay still.

"Good luck," Seamus whispered. "Don't do anything I wouldn't do."

"Thanks," Aisling whispered back. "See you."

She touched the wooden end of the stretcher superstitiously. If Seamus and the others were going to be taken to the police station, that left only Peter, Deirdre and herself against S.K.U.N.K. And Shavitov must really have it in for her now; there was no way he'd let her go if he caught her again. *Promising young Irish hockey-player throttled to death in Spanish back street!* She shivered, picked up the rucksack containing Mulligan and climbed quietly out of the ambulance after Deirdre and Peter.

"Now what?" she whispered.

"Let's get out of here."

☐

Fortunately the street was busy. Trying to look as if dropping out of the back of an ambulance which has been stopped by the police was something she did every evening, Aisling followed Deirdre across the pavement to mingle with the crowd. Peter came close behind them.

The policemen went back to their motorbikes, started their sirens, and escorted the ambulance down the street.

"Where do you think they're taking them?" Peter asked Deirdre.

"I don't know. We'll worry about that later, but first I have to make a phonecall. You speak a bit of Spanish, Peter. Can you ask someone where we can find a phone?"

"You can usually find one in a bar. Let's try that one over there." Peter pointed across the street to the Bar Gallego.

Three people were just coming out of it: two were men, one small and thin, the other big and fat, and the third person was a very plump woman.

Aisling and Peter pulled Deirdre behind a newspaper kiosk.

"What...?"

"It's Shavitov and Lerntowski!" Aisling whispered. She heard her voice trembling. It wasn't surprising, she thought: she felt weak all over. "They're with Antonia Browne!"

Deirdre peered round the side of the kiosk. "So *that's* why you call them Laurel and Hardy!"

Aisling pulled her back. "Don't let them see you!"

"It's all right, they're going the other way. Perhaps we should follow them. They might lead us to where they've hidden the flasks of nuclear waste."

Aisling wished she was back home in Sandycove. She wished Peter hadn't looked across the road just at that particular moment. She wished she could find an excuse to let him and Deirdre sort out S.K.U.N.K. while she found a nice friendly Irish consul and wept on his shoulder. Clasping the bag with Mulligan tightly to her chest, she sighed and joined the others as they tailed Shavitov, Lerntowski and Miss Browne through the town.

Fortunately, although it was very late, the streets

were teeming with people. "It's the *paseo*," Peter explained. "People in Spain eat their dinner much later than us and then they often go out for a walk afterwards."

"Thank goodness for that," Deirdre said. "It certainly makes acting the detective that much easier."

They followed the strange threesome through the old part of town, past beautiful houses with wrought-iron, glass-covered balconies (which reminded Aisling of some of the houses on the north side of Merrion Square back in Dublin—if only she was there!), and finally down a deserted street full of warehouses which led to the waterfront. Shavitov, Lerntowski and Miss Browne stopped in front of the door to one of the warehouses. A few seconds later the door opened and they disappeared inside.

"What do we do now?" Aisling asked.

"I think we should get the police," Peter suggested.

"The police?" Deirdre shook her head. "They've just arrested John Smith and Seamus, remember. Perry has them obeying his every wish like tame poodles."

"But this is different," Aisling argued. "Peregrine too wants to find out where S.K.U.N.K. has the waste flasks. Surely the important thing is to get to them before S.K.U.N.K. decides to move them? You heard Peregrine say that S.K.U.N.K. intends to take them to London and Paris and Bonn and then blow them up, didn't you? We can't afford to wait."

"I agree," Deirdre said. "We have to get help. But not necessarily from the police. You stay here and I'll ring the number I have for Greenpeace. They'll force the police to act and organise publicity. We want the world to know how easy it was to steal these flasks and how much harm could be done by them."

"I'm sure you do." The voice came from behind them. They spun round.

Standing behind them were the two ambulance men they'd last seen in Lourdes.

17

Run to Earth

"**D**on't, like, try anything funny, like," the fair-haired man warned. "This," he moved his hand in the pocket of his grubby white jacket so that something hard jutted out of it, pointing towards them, "...is a gun, like, and it's loaded. It's got, like, a silencer too—just in case you think anyone might notice a shot."

"Where...?" Aisling stuttered.

"Where did we come from?" the second man sneered. "Did you think the Boss didn't notice the three of you, tailing him across town like some sort of Famous Three in an Enid Blyton story? You must be thick."

"Rats," Aisling muttered. "Rats, rats and more rats." And they'd thought they'd been so clever.

"Move it!" the man with the gun ordered. "The Boss wants, like, to see you. Pronto."

Aisling looked at Peter. He shrugged. "Better do as he says."

"Get a move on!" The fair-haired man prodded Aisling and Peter towards the warehouse. The second man pushed Deirdre after them. Aisling looked round desperately but the alleyway was deserted. The main street was just a stone's throw away: she could hear the noise of traffic, but it might as well have been on the moon. She wondered, for a split second, whether it wouldn't be better to try to make a run for it and risk getting a bullet in her back. At least that would be quick. The thought of meeting Shavitov again tied her stomach up in a knot. She tried to make her legs run away but they wouldn't obey her. Trembling, she allowed herself to be pushed through the warehouse door with the others.

They were forced into a small office. Lerntowski, immaculate in a white suit and a white polo-necked jumper, was sitting in front of some sort of electronic machine, cleaning his nails with a nail file. He didn't look up. Shavitov was standing to his right, looking like a fat schoolboy who's been caught scribbling on walls by his headmaster. And beside Shavitov, her plump arm placed protectively around his huge shoulders, stood Antonia Browne, glaring at Lerntowski like a tigress defending her favourite cub.

Shavitov turned as they were brought in. His face was blank for a minute, and then it took on an expression of such hatred that Aisling felt it almost like a physical blow.

Miss Browne, on the other hand, seemed pleased to see her. "There you are, pet," she gushed. "I was very worried about you. I mean, I feel responsible to your godfather for you and when you rushed off in Santiago there, chicken, and Teddybear said we didn't have the time to wait for you, I felt very bad."

Aisling stared at her incredulously. Did she still not realise the sort of people she'd got herself mixed up with?

Lerntowski finally looked up from his long tapered fingers. "So we meet again," he squeaked in his high-pitched voice.

"I thought you were dead," Aisling heard herself stuttering. "We saw the *Fafnir* being torpedoed in Iceland; there was no way anyone could have survived."

"What is it you English (I do beg your pardon, Irish) say?" Lerntowski sneered. "'Do not count your chickens before they are born.' If you want to kill someone, you do not leave them a lifeline: you forgot to untie the dinghy from the *Fafnir*'s stern."

Aisling saw again the horrendous scene she had watched from the cliff-top in Iceland as the Viking ship, the *Fafnir*, blazed from prow to stern. It had been the twilight of an Icelandic late-summer midnight and a storm was approaching, shadowing the sea. She supposed it was possible that a dinghy could have left the blazing wreck without them noticing. It must have happened, otherwise neither Shavitov nor Lerntowski would be here now.

"So," Lerntowski went on. "You are trying to interfere with S.K.U.N.K. again. I am tempted to allow my colleague here to get rid of you, permanently this time, in any way he wants to. And," Lerntowski smiled coldly, "I'm sure he will make it as painful as possible for you. But should I give him this pleasure? I ask myself. He has been very naughty. He and this...woman," Lerntowski's high voice emphasised the word disapprovingly, "have tried to fool me, Lerntowski. That is unacceptable."

Shavitov hung his head again and stared at the rough wooden floor.

"Teddybear and I love each other," Miss Browne said firmly. "You can't stop us."

Lerntowski made a strange neighing sound which Aisling recognised as laughter. "Teddybear!" he said scornfully. "Love!" He looked at Shavitov. "For this, I should have you killed as well, my friend."

Please do, Aisling wished silently.

"Instead, I shall forgive you this time. Take these interfering busybodies to the ship. The world has not taken our threat seriously and it is time we showed what we can do."

"What can you do?" Deirdre asked, apparently innocently.

Lerntowski couldn't resist the chance to show off. "We have one flask of spent nuclear fuel in London, one in Bonn and one in Paris. Each has an explosive device attached to it. These can be set off by radio waves from this transmitter here. I shall give the world one last warning tonight and, if they still ignore me: boom! Tomorrow I explode one device, the cover of the flask cracks, the cooling fluid comes out and the rods inside heat up again, causing a fire it will not be easy to put out. You see, I have studied my nuclear physics."

"What happens when they go on fire?" Aisling asked, not sure if she wanted to know.

Lerntowski's thin features screwed up into a smile. "Radiation pours out, of course, little girl," he squeaked enthusiastically. "Radiation which will spread through the Houses of Parliament, the Bundeshaus in Bonn or the Assemblée Nationale in Paris, whichever one I decide to target first. And if they ignore the first one, I shall explode the second flask. I do not think I shall need the third."

His whole face was lit up, his cold eyes gleaming, his mouth twisted in an evil smile. He's mad, Aisling thought. Stark staring mad. Someone has to stop him.

"But that is enough questions," he went on. "You will not see what happens. You will be just three more dead bodies in the Bay of Biscay to be eaten by the little fishes. Take them out!"

The two ambulance men prodded Aisling, Peter and Deirdre into line with their guns. Miss Browne frowned at the men, as if they were a pair of little children who were being especially naughty. Then she stomped over to Lerntowski's desk. She leant her great bosom over it and looked down at him. "You are an evil little man," she said. "How can you even think such a thing? Don't you realise that people could be killed by all that radiation? God sees what you are doing, you know. He won't allow you to do this. You'd better stop right now and tell Him you're sorry."

Lerntowski drew back fastidiously. "You are a stupid woman," he hissed quietly. He turned to the ambulance men. "Take her away with the others."

Miss Browne appealed to Shavitov. "Stop them, Teddybear."

Shavitov continued to look at the floor as if studying for a degree in carpentry.

Lerntowski said something sharply to Shavitov in their own language. He jumped, went red and grabbed Miss Browne's arm, which he then twisted behind her back.

"Teddybear! What are you doing, chicken? That hurts!"

Shavitov shut his eyes, as if by not seeing her, he wouldn't hear her. "You shuts up, no?" he growled.

"Teddybear?" Miss Browne's voice trembled. "Why are you speaking to me like this?"

Shavitov opened his eyes again. "Valk!" he ordered. "Valk or I breaks your arm. And no more talkings, yes? No...more...talkings." He twisted her arm at each word so that she winced. Aisling began to feel sorry for her.

"Move!" the fair-haired ambulance man ordered the rest of them.

Aisling looked at the other two. Deirdre shrugged. "What choice have we?" she asked quietly.

"You at least are sensible, young lady," Lerntowski squeaked. "There is no point in making your end any more painful than it has to be. Now, all of you get out of here. I have work to do."

He turned his back to them and started to twiddle with the knobs on his machine. "S.K.U.N.K. calling London," she heard him squeak as they were hustled out of the warehouse. "S.K.U.N.K. calling London. This is a last warning..."

The alleyway was still deserted. They were forced to cross the quay to a fishing boat, which was bobbing innocently up and down in the circle of light cast on the black water by an overhead lamp. Deirdre was pushed on board first, then Peter. Aisling was just stepping on to the gangplank when she heard Miss Browne struggling with Shavitov behind her.

"I am not going on board that dirty trawler, Teddybear. I have to find my ladies again. Goodness knows what has happened to them. Really, pet, I am very disappointed in you. When I think how I have misled these dear old ladies, how I've dragged them all the way to Spain and now abandoned them in Santiago, and all for you...I knew it was wrong, but I *loved* you, Teddybear!"

Aisling realised they were all waiting to hear what Shavitov would reply: Peter and Deirdre and the first ambulance man in the boat, she and the second ambulance man on the quay. Stealthily, with her back turned to the man with the gun, she opened her holdall. Mulligan, delighted to get some fresh air again, poked his head out. Aisling pretended to drop the bag and bent to pick it up, wondering if the man behind her would shoot. He waited for her to stand up again, his attention still caught up in Antonia's appeal to Shavitov.

"Didn't you ever love me one teensie weensie bit, Teddybear?" she asked tearfully.

Shavitov mumbled something.

"What, pet?"

Mulligan was right out of the bag now. Aisling pushed him towards Shavitov's large black boots.

"Eet vas rrong to loves you, my darrling," Shavitov said slowly. "Lerntowski, he says...ACHOO!" And Shavitov suddenly started to stagger around the quay, sneezing explosively.

Aisling seized her chance. As Shavitov swayed between her and the ambulance man and Miss Browne looked on in alarm, she scooped up Mulligan and ran.

"Hey! Come back!" Shots rang out behind her. She kept on running. The shots stopped. She risked a quick glance over her shoulder and saw Miss Browne struggling with the ambulance man on the quay. Shavitov, doubled up and still sneezing, was shielding her from the second ambulance man in the boat.

"Good old Mulligan." She gave him a squeeze. "You've done it again!"

18

Reinforcements

A isling found herself back in the centre of town. Now what? She had to get help, but could she risk going to the police after they'd arrested John Smith, Seamus and Florence? She hoped Seamus and the others were all right: *Elderly Irish artist and his sister, together with Dalkey bookseller, languish in Spanish jail...*It might be better, she thought, to try someone else first. She remembered that Deirdre had wanted to get in touch with the Spanish branch of Greenpeace. But she hadn't their address and she didn't even speak Spanish: how on earth was she going to find them?

She sat down on a bench, still breathless from running so fast, and hugged Mulligan tightly. He growled, squeezed out of her arms and disappeared behind the nearest tree. There was a sound of scratching and then he came back again, jumped back on to her lap and started to wash himself.

"I'm glad you're here, Mulligan," Aisling whispered to him. "I only wish you could tell me what we ought to do now."

Mulligan stuck his nose into her face and gave her a quick lick.

"That's a lovely cat you have there!"

The voice was Irish. Aisling looked up. Three students were standing on the pavement, smiling down at her.

"Sorry." A tall boy, his dark hair drawn back into a ponytail, put his arm round the girl who had spoken. "Siobhán's just crazy about cats—*a mi novia le gustan mucho los gatos*."

The girl, whose hair was shaved apart from a ponytail at the top as orange as Mulligan's fur, bent down and tickled Mulligan under the chin. He purred like a dentist's drill.

"He's a dote," she said. "*Es precioso*."

Aisling hesitated. Could S.K.U.N.K. have sent them after her? She told herself she was going paranoid: they were obviously Irish. So what? the other half of her brain asked suspiciously; they could still belong to S.K.U.N.K.! She shook her head, like a dog trying to dislodge an annoying flea, and decided to trust them. After all, she was never going to be able to save the others, let alone the world, all by herself.

"Can you help me?" she asked. "I need to find someone in Greenpeace."

"Hey, you're Irish! What are you doing sitting here all alone with a cat in the middle of the night?"

"It's a long story," Aisling said wearily. "I'll tell you about it later. At the moment I really need to find someone in Greenpeace. It's a matter of life and death."

The other boy grinned. His head was completely shaven and his earrings were as long and dangly as the girl they called Siobhán's. "I know the world's in a mess," he said, "but I didn't think things were that desperate. Or are we finally going to destroy the planet tonight?"

Aisling appealed to the girl. At least she liked cats—
maybe she'd understand. "It's very important. I have to
find someone to help us."

She was right. Siobhán took her seriously. "We'll help
you," she said. "Are you lost? Can you remember the
hotel your parents are in?"

"I've got to find someone from Greenpeace," Aisling
repeated. "Or..." she thought quickly, "a newspaper we
can trust."

"You're not joking, are you?" Siobhán asked. "What's
happening?"

Aisling thought of telling them about S.K.U.N.K. and
the warehouse, and about Peter and Deirdre being
prisoners on the boat. But, even if they believed her,
which was hardly likely, they wouldn't be able to help.
"You speak Spanish," she said. "How can I get in touch
with..."

"We know, Greenpeace," grinned the first student. "It
seems the lady's got a one-track mind. Anyone any ideas
how we can help her?"

"Maruja's into environmental issues, isn't she?" the
skinhead suggested. "We could try her."

"Come on, then."

They led Aisling down a side-street and up a long
flight of stairs to a tiny attic room.

"*Hola, Maruja!*" the long-haired boy shouted through
the door. "*Somos Conor y Mark y Siobhán. Tenemos que
hablar contigo.*"

A beautiful dark-haired girl appeared. Fortunately she
spoke English. Even more fortunately, she actually knew
Deirdre from international environmental meetings.

When Aisling told her story, to the astonished gasps and amazed whistles of the Irish students, she didn't bother asking unnecessary questions but acted immediately.

"I am going down to phone. You say this Lerntowski man intends to set off a device in London if he does not get an answer tonight? And that your friends have been kidnapped and are going to be murdered at sea? Then we must involve the police."

"But they arrested John Smith and Seamus. They're working for..." She hesitated. She hadn't had time to wonder why the police had stopped the ambulance. Could it just have been because John Smith had been speeding? (*Had* he been speeding?) Or could they have been S.K.U.N.K. agents disguised as policemen? Or were they, as Deirdre had thought, protecting the interests of the nuclear industry?

Maruja seemed to have read her thoughts. "If the police know what is happening, they have no doubt been asked by the government to make sure nobody else finds out. The nuclear fuel industry doesn't want another scandal on its hands, *verdad*? But they must stop what did you call that organisation? S.K.U.N.K.? Otherwise no one will be safe. So, if we tell them, they will act."

"And the nuclear industry will get away with it again," the long-haired student complained. "What it is to have money and power."

"Not necessarily, Conor," Maruja said quietly. "I shall go now and phone the police, but I shall also phone some journalist friends. We must make sure that S.K.U.N.K. is stopped, but we must also make sure that this matter is not, how do you say? quietened up. You all wait here—

173

I won't be long. Why don't you cook the poor little girl some supper, you three? And then maybe you should rest, *niña*. You look worn out."

Aisling didn't feel hungry—unlike Mulligan. As soon as Conor opened the fridge door, he leapt out of Aisling's arms, streaked across the floor and tried to hurl himself inside the fridge. The girl called Siobhán laughed, pulled him back and broke an egg into a saucer. He wolfed it down, licked the plate clean and looked up at her expectantly. She poured him a bowl of milk and cut a piece of hard Spanish sausage for him. He dragged it under the table and started to chew.

Conor grinned as he scrambled together eggs, tomatoes, cold potatoes, cooked onions and sausage to make a Spanish omelette on Maruja's tiny stove. "That cat sounds like a pride of lions slavering over a dead wildebeest!"

Aisling's appetite returned at the sight of the food, even though she was so tired that she could hardly keep awake.

"Why don't you lie down," Siobhán suggested, when they had eaten. "We'll wake you when Maruja comes back."

Aisling curled up on Maruja's narrow bed and Mulligan snuggled down under the covers beside her. She stroked his orange head. Thank goodness she'd brought him: even here, where she felt she was amongst friends at last, he was better than a comfort blanket. She hoped Maruja was sorting things out and that the police would be quick. Shavitov's temper must be worse than ever, now that she'd used Mulligan to start up his allergy again and help her to escape; and Deirdre and Peter were his prisoners and completely at his mercy!

□

The next thing she knew, someone was shaking her awake. The room seemed full of people. Had S.K.U.N.K. found out where she was and come for her?

"It's all right, Aisling." Conor smiled reassuringly at her. "It's only a couple of journalists. They want to hear your story."

"You should have let her sleep," Siobhán complained. "She's obviously exhausted, poor thing."

"There is no time," Maruja said in her strong Spanish accent. "The police are surrounding the warehouse. We have to tell the world what is happening."

Aisling sat up. "Of course," she said. "What do you want to know?"

There were two journalists, one male, one female. The male one was called Rodriguez and worked for a Spanish newspaper; the woman, Joan, was American. Aisling told them everything she knew about the nuclear waste rods, how S.K.U.N.K. had managed to swap three flasks of them for dummy flasks on a carrier travelling from Italy to England, and how S.K.U.N.K. was now threatening the world.

"Are they dangerous, these things?" the Spanish reporter asked.

Aisling repeated what Lerntowski had said: if the flasks were punctured, the fluid which kept the red-hot fuel rods cool would escape and the rods would go on fire, starting a huge conflagration and releasing a horrendous amount of radiation.

"We'd better go down to the harbour, then, and see what's happening," the American reporter said. "Come on, you guys."

□

Aisling led them back to the warehouse. The alleyway was blocked by police vehicles. They tried to approach along the quay, but it was roped off too. So they joined a crowd of curious passers-by and watched.

A policeman with a loudhailer was shouting something at the warehouse in Spanish. Then he changed to English. "You are surrounded! Come out or we shall come in and get you."

Suddenly Lerntowski's squeaky voice resounded across the quay. He was obviously using some sort of loudspeaker or radio equipment. "If you try to come in, I shall set off the nuclear devices I have prepared. You will have the destruction of the parliaments of Britain, Germany and France on your conscience!"

"At least there won't be anyone working in any of the parliament buildings at this time of night," Aisling whispered.

"There will. There's an important bill being discussed in Westminster, for example, so there's bound to be an all-night sitting," Joan told her quietly. "And the effects of radiation will linger on for months, if not years."

"Wait!" the policeman shouted. "We are prepared to bargain with you. What are your conditions?"

Conor tugged at Aisling's arm. "Look up there! Isn't that two men on the roof? Do you think they're trying to get in?"

"I hope so," Aisling said fervently.

Conor was right. The policeman kept Lerntowski talking while the two dark figures disappeared through a skylight in the roof. The crowd waited in absolute silence, holding its breath. Lerntowski demanded that the British, French and German governments paid S.K.U.N.K. ten billion pounds. The policeman said he was trying to get in touch with them but it would take a little while longer.

And then the speaker Lerntowski had used sounded again. But this time, it was a Spanish voice which spoke.

"They've caught him!" Maruja said. *"Gracias a Dios!"*

The crowd surged forwards to see what would happen next.

Aisling was suddenly aware of a fishing boat pulling out from the quay.

"Shavitov's getting away!" she shouted. "And he's got Peter and Deirdre with him. We have to stop them!"

19

The Chase

Aisling, still clutching Mulligan, followed Maruja as she pushed through the crowd to the nearest policeman. She listened anxiously as Maruja explained about the fishing boat, trying to understand what she was saying. The policeman seemed to be equally mystified: his expression became more and more doubtful as Maruja went on.

She threw her hands in the air and turned to Aisling. "Tell him," she said in English. "Tell him you saw your friends being kidnapped."

"No entiendo inglés," the policeman muttered, before Aisling had even spoken.

Aisling looked back at the harbour: the fishing boat had almost reached open sea. "You have to help!" she pleaded. "He'll kill them!"

Maruja tried again. *"Su jefe? Tengo que hablar con su jefe."* She pronounced it "heffey": Aisling guessed it meant chief.

The policeman shrugged. Then he took out a two-way radio and said a few words into it. He turned to Maruja. *"Ya viene el jefe,"* he said.

"His boss is coming," Maruja interpreted, and sure enough, a higher-ranking policeman pushed his way through the crowd towards them.

Maruja explained again. The Inspector turned to Aisling. "This is true? The colleague of the man we have arrested is kidnapping your friends?"

"Yes. They're on that fishing boat out there!" The boat was almost out of sight. "We've got to get to them before Shavitov kills them!"

The Inspector patted her on the head, like a child. "Do not worry, *niña*. We will save your friends." He, too, took out a radio and gave a few curt orders into it.

Policemen pushed the crowd back until the quay was cleared. A police car screamed towards them and stopped. The Inspector helped Aisling and Maruja in to it, jumped in himself and the car roared off, its siren screaming.

"What's happening?" Aisling asked, her heart thumping against Mulligan's orange fur. "Are they going to arrest us?"

The Inspector turned round and looked at her suspiciously. "Should we arrest you? You are not playing a hoax, I hope?"

"No. It's just that..." She tailed off in embarrassment: she couldn't very well tell him that Seamus and Florence had already been arrested along with John Smith and were probably still in a Spanish jail right now. "It's just that I was worried that you didn't believe us," she finished lamely.

The Inspector continued to look at her doubtfully.

"Shavitov is in that boat with Peter and Deirdre," she insisted. "And I know he's going to kill them if nobody stops him in time. He's mad that we've messed things up again and he'll take it out on them, I know he will."

The Inspector seemed to believe her. "There are some others on board?" he asked.

"Two gorillas..."

He raised an eyebrow. He was extremely handsome, Aisling thought: *Irish schoolgirl elopes with Spanish policeman!* She gave herself a mental shake. "Two bullies from S.K.U.N.K.," she explained. "They're both armed. Oh, and there's Antonia Browne as well." Aisling had forgotten about her. Maybe Miss Browne would stop Shavitov from hurting Peter and Deirdre? She crossed her fingers.

"Antonia Browne?"

"She's in love with Shavitov. But I don't think she has anything to do with S.K.U.N.K."

"I see. Well, I tell you now what we have planned. We are going to an airfield not far from here. I have asked for a helicopter to be made ready for us. I have also told a police ship to follow your ship from La Coruña. Between the two of us, we shall stop your friends from coming to harm. So cheer up, *niña*. It will be all okay."

Aisling smiled back at him but she still kept her fingers crossed and held on tightly to Mulligan. She'd seen how angry Shavitov could be when she'd got in his way in the past; now that Lerntowski had been captured and he was all alone, he'd be madder than ever. He was capable of any cruelty and, no matter how much she hoped differently, she didn't really believe Miss Browne could save Deirdre and Peter from his vengeance. They just had to get there in time.

□

They left the town behind and sped through the dark countryside, the police car's headlights illuminating stone walls, turning the road into a tunnel under overhanging bushes, spotlighting for an instant granite houses and granaries, transforming the eyes of startled animals into fiery jewels. Aisling hoped the airport wasn't much further. Please, please let us be in time, she prayed. She wished she had as much faith in prayer as the elderly ladies on their pilgrimage to Lourdes: Peter and Deirdre needed all the help they could get.

They reached a small airfield where a helicopter was waiting for them. Aisling, still clutching Mulligan, climbed on board; to her surprise, nobody tried to stop her. Three policemen were already in the helicopter, as well as the pilot, but there were two empty seats. She sat down in one and the Inspector took the other. She looked back: Maruja had stayed by the police car.

They took off, swaying into the air and making more noise than Aisling would have thought possible. She looked down. Tiny pinpricks of light shone from cottages beneath, a car's headlights moved across the black countryside like a glow-worm, and then they were over the sea whose heaving darkness gleamed irregularly when the moon flashed between scudding clouds. How were they ever going to find Shavitov and the fishing boat in that dark immensity?

The pilot flicked a switch and a spotlight underneath the helicopter suddenly threw a large circle of light on the sea below. The Inspector peered out of his window. Aisling looked out on her side but saw nothing except heaving black waves.

Suddenly, a fishing boat without lights was caught in the beam like a dancer in a spotlight on the stage.

The pilot said something into his microphone and then shouted to the Inspector. The Inspector nodded and the helicopter started to descend.

It hovered over the fishing boat. Aisling could see two men on deck: the fair-haired ambulance man and Shavitov. There was no sign of either Peter or Deirdre. She crossed her fingers again and hoped that they were still alive.

The ambulance man had a machine gun and was aiming it at the helicopter. She ducked back down out of view. Bullets pinged on the fuselage and the spotlight went out. The pilot swore in Spanish and jerked the helicopter higher again.

"Now what?" Aisling wondered.

The Inspector pointed downwards. A shaft of light was piercing the darkness, travelling across the water towards them. Then the moon came out and she could see that it belonged to a second boat, obviously the police launch the Inspector had spoken of.

It was like watching a film: the fishing boat, a dark shape on the water, continued in a straight line beneath them while the police launch slowly gained on it.

Then the spotlight from the launch reached the fishing boat, illuminating its deck once more. She saw Shavitov disappear into the cabin. As the ambulance man knelt in the stern and fired at the launch, he came out on deck again, dragging a figure, either Peter or Deirdre, Aisling couldn't see which.

The Inspector had obviously seen him too. He snapped

an order to the pilot and the helicopter descended once more. One of the men behind her opened the door and let down a rope ladder. Now she could hear the firing beneath them. She shuddered.

The moon went behind a cloud again, but the launch was close enough for them to see the fishing boat clearly, bright in the launch's spotlight. Sure enough, Shavitov was on deck with...Aisling peered down...Deirdre. Then another figure joined him, a figure almost as large as his own. It must be Antonia Browne, she thought. Miss Browne seemed to be arguing with him.

The ambulance man at the stern was still firing at the police launch. Someone behind the spotlight started to fire back. The ambulance man staggered and fell.

"*Ya!*" ordered the Inspector in the helicopter. The helicopter swooped down to hover directly over the boat; one of the men shinned down the ladder and jumped on to the deck; the other two followed immediately. The second ambulance man rushed out of the cabin, holding a machine gun. There was another burst of gunfire and the light from the police launch went out, leaving everything in darkness again. Aisling wondered what was happening. The Inspector swore and started down the rope ladder too. Aisling was left in the helicopter with Mulligan and the pilot.

She dumped Mulligan on the seat beside her and went to the door. She peered down. She could see the dim form of the boat beneath her: figures milled about; guns flashed. Mulligan came and stood beside her. He rubbed himself against the back of her legs, sniffed, and gave a plaintive *prriau*.

Without stopping to think, Aisling started to climb down the ladder. The rope spun round and Aisling spun with it. She tried to imagine she was back at school, climbing down one of the ropes in the gym: *Schoolgirl gymnast wins international rope-climbing competition!* But there you had a mattress on the floor to catch you if you fell: here she only had the dark shadow of the fishing boat beneath her. She decided not to look down again.

The moon came through a gap in the clouds just as her feet hit the deck.

"Velcome to ze party, leetle girl." She wheeled round. Shavitov was grinning at her, a machine gun in his hands. He had herded two policemen and the Inspector into a huddle beside the cabin with Deirdre and Peter. She looked for the two ambulance men and the other policeman: behind Shavitov, three dark shapes were slumped on the deck. Antonia Browne was bending over them.

She straightened up. "They're dead, pet," she said accusingly. "And it's all your fault. Really, Teddybear, you must learn to control your temper. You've gone much too far this time."

"Be quiet, my loves," Shavitov muttered, not moving his eyes from Aisling and the others. "Trust me. All vill be vells."

"You cannot get away with this," the Inspector said firmly. "You are outnumbered. My men in the launch will be on board in a minute."

Aisling risked a glance over the side of the fishing boat. Sure enough, the police launch was alongside.

"You hears me, Spanish policemen?" Shavitov bellowed

suddenly. "You in ze boat? Eef you makes one move to come on my sheep, I keels everyvon here. You understands? Everyvons."

Someone in the launch shouted to the Inspector.

"*Esperad! Con cuidado!*" he shouted back.

Had he asked them to be cautious? Aisling wondered. Was Shavitov going to be allowed to get away with it?

Suddenly, a dark shape fell out of the sky onto Shavitov's broad shoulders. He gave a yelp, jumped back, dropped his machine gun as if it were red-hot and started to claw at his neck. "ACHOO!" he went. "A...A...A... ACHOO!"

The Inspector dived for the machine gun. His two colleagues grabbed Shavitov, struggled with him as his body was convulsed in gigantic sneezes, and finally managed to snap a pair of handcuffs round his immense wrists.

Mulligan jumped off Shavitov's neck, ignored the rest of them and scrambled down into the hold of the ship. Aisling grinned at Deirdre and Peter. "Good old Mulligan. I'll bet there's still some fish down there. He must have smelt it from the helicopter."

"He saved our lives again," Peter said admiringly. "When we get back to shore, I'm going to buy him all the fish in La Coruña."

"He's an incredible animal," Deirdre agreed. "I've never seen a cat climb down a rope ladder before."

"If he's hungry, he's capable of anything," Aisling said proudly.

From deep in the hold of the ship came the sound of fishbones being crunched.

185

20
Reunion

S oon the fishing boat was swarming with policemen. They removed the bodies and transferred Shavitov and Miss Browne into the police launch. The Inspector turned to Aisling, Peter and Deirdre.

"My men, they will bring this fishing boat back to the harbour," he shouted above the noise of the helicopter which was still hovering above the ship. "Would you three like to come back in the helicopter with me?"

"Prima!" Peter was delighted. "I've always wanted to fly in a helicopter."

"Just wait till I get Mulligan," Aisling said. She knelt down beside the hold. "Mulligan! Come on, Mulligan! You must be full by now."

"Who is this Mulligan?" the Inspector asked. "Was he also a prisoner?"

"He's Seamus's cat," Peter explained. "And he's down there somewhere."

"Ah. The cat. One minute." The Inspector rapped out an order to one of his policemen. A torch was produced and shone into the almost-empty hold. Mulligan, crouched over the remains of a cod in the far corner, looked up, his yellow eyes glowing in the reflected light.

Aisling sighed. "I'd better go and get him," she said. Gingerly, she climbed down the iron ladder at the edge of the hold, grabbed Mulligan, who growled protestingly and dug his claws into the fish he'd been chewing, pulled the fish out of his grasp and lugged him back up on deck.

The Inspector peered closely at the large orange cat. "How did that get down there?" he asked.

Mulligan put out a sandpapery tongue, smelling strongly of dead fish, and licked the Inspector's nose.

He quickly stepped out of reach. "Do you want to bring him back in the helicopter too?" He didn't sound particularly delighted with the idea.

"He saved our lives," Deirdre said. "We can't leave him behind."

Aisling looked up at the rope ladder. The helicopter was quite low: it wasn't that far. And she didn't fancy going back in the launch with Shavitov, even if he had been handcuffed, or on the fishing boat by herself. "Fine," she said. "No problem."

The Inspector smiled at her. He really did look like a film-star, Aisling thought dreamily. "All right then," he said. "Just hold the rope and my men will pull you up."

Aisling didn't feel exactly dignified as she was pulled up into the helicopter like a fish at the end of a line, but at least Mulligan stayed still and didn't struggle.

Peter and Deirdre followed them up, and the Inspector came last. He pulled the ladder in, shut the door and the helicopter headed back to the airport.

To Aisling's surprise, a taxi was waiting for them on the tarmac. There was also a small crowd of people by the helicopter pad. She felt the skin crawl at the back of her neck. Had Lerntowski escaped? Was he waiting for them with more gangsters from S.K.U.N.K.?

She relaxed as she realised it was only Maruja, the three Irish students and the two journalists. The driver of the police car was standing slightly to one side, keeping a disapproving eye on them.

As the Inspector started to speak angrily to Maruja, the others crowded round Aisling, Deirdre and Peter.

"How did you get here?" Aisling asked. "We left you in La Coruña."

Conor grinned. "We got a taxi and followed you. In true Agatha Christie style."

"Tell us what happened out there," Joan, the American journalist, asked urgently.

"Shavitov's been caught by the police," Peter explained. "He's being taken back to La Coruña with Miss Browne. I think the gangsters who were with him are both dead. And at least one policeman is too."

"What about Lerntowski?" Aisling asked. "Did he manage to set off any of the waste fuel containers? Are London and Bonn and Paris still okay?"

"As far as we know, yes. We've been listening to the news, and nothing seems to have happened. Although," Joan smiled wryly, "if there has been a nuclear accident in Westminster or the Bundeshaus or wherever, it's not the kind of thing they would broadcast to the world."

"We have informed our papers of everything you said to us," Rodriguez said quickly. "We hope they are following it up."

The Police Inspector came over. *"No tienen derecho a estar aquí,"* he rapped out. "You have no right to be here."

"We're just friends of Aisling," Joan said. "We were worried about her."

The Inspector frowned. "Aisling, you will come with me to headquarters. I need you to make a...what do you call it? a statement. And your two friends who were on the ship. And perhaps you, too, señorita," he said to Maruja, "as interpreter. The rest of you must go."

"Sure, Sir." Joan smiled at the others. "See you, Aisling. Come on, Rodriguez, let's get out of here."

Aisling was surprised that the two journalists left so meekly. As she travelled back into town, crammed in the back seat of the police car with Maruja, Deirdre and Peter, she wondered if she'd ever see her Irish friends or the journalists again. She remembered the last time they'd all been together, outside the warehouse. She hoped Lerntowski had been stopped before he could put his threat into action, but if he had, then at least nobody could hush it up.

Or could they? she wondered. Could Joan be right? The government would probably come up with some reasonable excuse (like a terrorist attack) and nobody would ever know about the waste flasks being stolen and how dangerous they were. She hoped the papers Joan and Rodriguez reported for had believed them—but would they want to hush it up too?

They pulled up outside the police station and the Inspector led them inside.

To Aisling's surprise, Peregrine rushed towards them.

"Deirdre! Thank goodness you're all right! I was dreadfully worried about you!"

"Hello, Peregrine." Deirdre looked at him coolly. "You wouldn't know where John is, would you? And Florence and Seamus?"

"They're here."

"I thought they might be."

"They're really quite safe." Peregrine sounded defensive. "I made sure they were given a cell to themselves and a decent supper."

"Then perhaps you can make equally sure that they get out of that cell now." Deirdre smiled so sweetly at Peregrine that Aisling almost felt sorry for him.

He blushed.

"What is all this about?" the Inspector asked. "You are speaking too fast..."

Peregrine turned to him. *"Los persones...en la...er... cella..."*

Maruja spoke to the Inspector in Spanish.

"What did you say?" Aisling whispered.

"I told him your godfather and the others were also fighting S.K.U.N.K. and have been arrested by mistake."

"Can we see them?" Aisling asked.

The Inspector issued a string of orders and two constables rushed out.

"What's happening?" Aisling asked Maruja.

"Just wait."

Footsteps sounded in the corridor outside, the door opened and Florence and John Smith stepped into the room.

"Aisling! Thank goodness you're all right! I was quite worried about you. And Peter and Deirdre too! Really, you children shouldn't be up at this time of night. You should both be in bed."

Aisling went over and gave Florence a warm hug. "It's great to see you again. Are you okay? And how's Seamus?"

"Not in the best of tempers," John Smith answered for her. "In fact, if language could drill holes in solid granite, we'd have been out of here ages ago. If he'd had an encyclopedia, now, to occupy his mind, he wouldn't have been quite so frustrated, but you will insist on travelling without one."

Deirdre grinned. "Has John been boring you to death all this time?" she asked Florence.

"I think perhaps Seamus will be glad to leave," Florence said tactfully.

The Inspector interrupted. "All right. Enough of this talk. Perhaps you will tell me now what all this excitement is about."

When they had explained everything that had happened, Aisling asked the question she'd been dying to ask. "Did Lerntowski have time to burst open any of the flasks?"

"Actually no, Aisling." Peregrine sounded very pleased with himself. "We were frightfully lucky and just managed to stop him in time. We've since been in contact with the governments in London, Paris and Bonn and the flasks are being carefully removed and will be returned to England. Nobody will know they were ever stolen at all."

"We do," Aisling pointed out.

"And we'll make sure the newspapers do, too," Florence said firmly. "It is disgraceful the way these things were left lying about like that!"

"They were not left lying about like that, as you put it," Peregrine said angrily. "They were stored under the utmost security. There should have been absolutely no danger at all. If S.K.U.N.K. hadn't stolen them from the carrier..."

"Exactly," Deirdre said. "And if S.K.U.N.K. can do it today, someone else will be able to do it tomorrow. We need to ban all nuclear transports in order to be safe. Do you realise what an accident to one of these carriers could mean? A nuclear explosion the size of Chernobyl!"

"But there cannot be such an accident. We really do take every precaution."

"I think the world should be allowed to judge for itself, don't you?" Deirdre suggested.

Peregrine sighed. "I'm afraid it can't, actually. This absolutely must be hushed up—you have to see that. Otherwise there'll be the most dreadful panic."

Florence looked at him disapprovingly. "I don't intend to hush it up, young man. As soon as I can make contact with a journalist, I shall tell him everything that has happened."

Peregrine smiled an apologetic little smile. "I'm afraid I'm absolutely going to have to insist that you sign the Official Secrets Act," he said.

"At gunpoint? Like you did before?" John Smith asked pleasantly.

Peregrine looked sheepish. "Well, actually, no. But you really do have to sign it; you must see that."

"You know you can't make us sign it," Deirdre said.

Peregrine looked at the Inspector.

"Do I take it you are threatening to lock all of us up

192

in a Spanish jail for the rest of our lives unless we sign your stupid piece of paper?" Florence glared at Peregrine just as Miss O'Keefe had glared at her in Junior School, Aisling thought, the time she'd let a box of snails loose in the classroom.

Peregrine blushed.

"Too many people know we're here, Perry," Deirdre said.

"And anyway, the papers have been told already," Aisling added.

Peregrine spun round. "What?"

"I told two journalists. They've already reported to their papers. You can't keep it quiet now."

There was a knock on the door.

"*Pase!*" shouted the Inspector.

A small policeman poked his head round the door. He rattled off something in Spanish.

"Good," Maruja said. "The police station is besieged by journalists. They want to talk to us."

The Inspector looked at Peregrine.

Peregrine looked at the others. "You mustn't speak to them!" he appealed.

Deirdre turned to the Inspector. "Can we go?" she asked. "Or is there anything else you want us to tell you?"

The Inspector shrugged.

Florence stood up. "Perhaps you will be so kind as to take me and Mr O'Toole to a good hotel," she suggested to the Inspector. She turned to the others. "Deirdre and her Spanish friend seem quite capable of dealing with the press, so I suggest you two young ones come with

193

me. You need your beauty sleep, you know, Aisling."

"We won't be long," Aisling said.

She certainly did not intend to miss this press conference. For the first time in her life, she was going to have the opportunity to talk to some real journalists and actually get her name in the papers at last. *Irish schoolgirl tells how S.K.U.N.K. threatened to irradiate the world!* With any luck it might make the front page of *The Irish Times*.

Louise would have to believe her now!

□□□

By the Same Author

The Door

Circling the Triangle

Anna's Six Wishes

Liza's Lamb

A Monster Called Charlie

Other books in the S.K.U.N.K. series:

S.K.U.N.K. and the Ozone Conspiracy

S.K.U.N.K. and the Splitting Earth

S.K.U.N.K. and the Freak Flood Fiasco

S.K.U.N.K. and the Bride of Dracula

Published by Poolbeg